I'M IN LOVE WITH A CHURCH GIRL

I'M IN LOVE WITH A CHURCH GIRL

A NOVEL

RYAN PHILLIPS

DESTINY IMAGE® PUBLISHERS, INC.

P.O. Box 310, Shippensburg, PA 17257-0310

"Promoting Inspired Lives."

This book and all other Destiny Image, Revival Press, MercyPlace, Fresh Bread, Destiny Image Fiction, and Treasure House books are available at Christian bookstores and distributors worldwide.

For a U.S. bookstore nearest you, call 1-800-722-6774.

For more information on foreign distributors, call 717-532-3040.

Reach us on the Internet: www.destinyimage.com.

ISBN 13 TP: 978-0-7684-0376-3

ISBN 13 Ebook: 978-0-7684-8439-7

For Worldwide Distribution, Printed in the U.S.A.

1 2 3 4 5 6 7 8 / 17 16 15 14 13

Part One

Easy, Breezy, Beautiful

1

"Go! Go! Go!" Miles laid on his car horn and willed the ambling red Prius in front of him to speed up. Craning his neck, he glimpsed the silver convertible Sebring he'd been chasing rest at a stop sign two blocks ahead, before it turned left and vanished behind a row of buildings. "Come on, man. Move out of the way!" Impatiently, he jerked his steering wheel and maneuvered his black Bentley around a string of cars stalled at a red light. Ignoring the traffic ahead, Miles pressed his foot on the accelerator and sped through the busy intersection, narrowly missing a minivan.

His tires screeched as he took a hard left onto First Street. Intently, he scanned the clot of cars around him. "Where are you?" he murmured, slowing his speed to better survey the side alleys and crowded parking lots. A surge of adrenaline coursed through his body like an electric shock the instant he spotted her in the distance. Following her with focused precision, he navigated his way through afternoon rush hour traffic. The restaurants and boutiques that lined downtown San Jose's pedestrian-littered sidewalks blended into a colorful blur of colors as he revved the engine and his speedometer crept past seventy.

Brazenly he blew through one stop sign, then another. "Gotcha!" he said, finally closing in on her. Miles rolled down his window, but before he could ease alongside her, he heard the unmistakable blare of a police siren. A glance in his rearview mirror revealed a black and white squad car, lights flashing, hot on his trail.

"Man, you gotta be kidding me!" Begrudgingly, he signaled right and pulled onto the shoulder of the road. A sinking sensation settled over Miles as the driver of the silver convertible continued on her way, seemingly unaware that she was even being followed.

Miles had only snatched a glimpse of his mystery woman as she'd driven by him a few minutes earlier. Cruising with her ragtop down, she hadn't noticed him—didn't even look his way. But for a moment, for one mesmerized second, his world stood still. She was beautiful. High cheek bones, full lips, and a delicately pointed chin. Her black hair, long and wavy, glistened in the California sun, as did her olive skin. And her eyes... well, he never saw them; they were hidden behind a pair of gold-rimmed sunglasses. But he imagined they were an intoxicating hazel—sultry and mysterious, just like her.

"You in a hurry today, son?" The officer's gruff voice snatched Miles from his thoughts. Miles shook his head, unwilling to meet the stern pair of eyes glaring at him through his open driver's side window.

"You wouldn't believe me if I told you," Miles said.

Cocking his head, the officer furled his lip into a mocking smirk. "Yeah. You're probably right. Driver's license, registration, and proof of insurance."

Miles reached for his glove box, but not before stealing one last peek at the silver convertible as it coasted across San Salvador Street and disappeared from sight.

~

"Is that you, Caesar?"

"No, Ma. It's me," Miles called out. He closed the front door and made his way through the familiar halls of his childhood home until he reached the kitchen. His mom was seated on one of the stools lined along the center island, casually flipping through a magazine. In the corner of the room, the evening news played quietly on a small television set. On the stove, two lidded pots bubbled, their contents filling the air with a delicious scent.

Julia Montego's face lit up with genuine delight at the sight of her son. "Now, this is a nice surprise! What are you doing here, baby?"

Miles greeted his mom with a kiss on the cheek and a warm embrace. "I just came by to put some paperwork in my safe," he said, gesturing at the leather duffle bag dangling from his shoulder. "I'll be right back, okay?"

She nodded and shooed him off with a playful wave of her hand.

Miles doubled back the way he came and cut through the den toward his old bedroom. The space had long since been turned into an office, where his father, a retired accountant, often withdrew in the evenings to enjoy a snifter of cognac and a good book. Miles made a beeline for the closet where he'd concealed the safe behind a shield of old coats. With several deft flicks of his wrist, he turned the combination dial on the metal door until it clicked open.

Inside, neatly wrapped bundles of cash rested in towering stacks along the safe's metal walls. Carefully Miles unzipped his duffle bag and slowly, methodically transferred another dozen bundles to his stash. When he was done, he shut the safe's heavy door—checking to make sure it was securely locked—and rejoined his mom in the kitchen.

"What you cookin' on?"

"Some spaghetti," she said distractedly, her eyes trained on the television. "I've always wanted to go there."

Miles followed her stare to the small screen across the room. A montage of a young couple scuba diving, relaxing by a crystal blue pool, and enjoying an al fresco candlelit dinner flickered across the screen. "Sandals Resorts?" he asked, pulling up a seat beside her. "So why don't you go?"

"Oh, sure. Like it's that easy." She cast Miles a teasing grin. "We're not all millionaires like you, mister."

"Stop it," he said, bashful, but proud. It was true. Miles' business acumen, coupled with his undeniable charisma and raw hustle had made him a very wealthy man. Over the years, he'd had his hands in many enterprises—some more above board than others—and, as a result, he'd amassed a small fortune by his thirties.

"So how you doin', baby?" Julia asked.

"I'm good. In fact, I'm extra good."

"Extra good, huh?" Julia's warm gaze searched his face and Miles smiled. His mom was timeless. At sixty-three, she still retained the same youthful glow she had when he was a kid—the same deep-set brown eyes, wide smile, and button nose. The same regal posture, infectious laugh, and wickedly brilliant sense of humor. More often than not, she wore her shoulder-length curls in a simple French twist or a dainty chignon. Her elegance was undeniable, yet understated, and eclipsed only by her sweet nature and kind heart.

She was, and had always been, his strongest supporter and biggest motivator. In her own career, Julia Montego had climbed the ranks from a lowly sales associate to a district manager for one of the largest clothing outlets in the San Francisco Bay area. Through word and deed, she'd instilled in Miles the unshakable certainty that hard work and determination were two keys that would grant him access to any door he chose to open in life.

Though retired for nearly two years now, Julia showed no signs of mellowing. She ran her house with the same straight-nose, matter-of-fact approach she'd used to run her stores and often channeled her trademark brand of bulldogged persistence—once reserved for boardroom talks and contract negotiations—when she wanted to persuade her husband to do something or felt the need to pester Miles, yet again, about finally settling down and starting a family.

As if on cue, she asked, "Well, Mr. Extra Good, when are you going to give me a grandchild?"

Miles laughed. "There you go again talking 'bout these grandkids. Look, Ma. I told you. Don't be expecting no grandkids from me anytime soon."

"Why not?" Before he could answer, she wagged a slender finger at him. "You need to come to church with me and find yourself a good woman there."

Miles shrugged. He could admit that he'd been with a fair share of women in his time. He could also admit that none of them met his mom's standard of "good." A vision of the mystery woman he'd lost downtown suddenly flashed into his mind. Miles shook the vision from his head.

"Church, huh?" He chuckled at the thought of himself seated in a pew, dressed in his Sunday best. The image was so far from who he was, from who he wanted to be.

"What Miles? You act like you weren't raised in church. I took you every week."

"Yeah, and I was bored every week, Ma." He thought back, with a shudder, to the endless Sundays of long liturgies, gloomy music, and spooky statues. "I don't know. Maybe the whole God thing just isn't for me."

"God is for everybody," she said, knitting her brows. "Don't forget that, Miles. You have a lot to be grateful for."

Sensing a lecture coming, Miles took his mom's hand in his and gave it a squeeze. "I know I do," he said. "Starting with you."

Despite herself, her expression softened. "Always a charmer."

"What can I say?" Miles rose from his seat. "I get it from my ma." Gently pulling her from her chair, he gave her a warm hug.

"You staying for dinner?"

"No, I gotta head out." Miles grabbed the empty duffel bag at his feet. "But, I'll tell you what. Next Sunday, if you happen to come across one of those nice young ladies at your church, give her my number and tell her I'm down for whatever."

"Whatever, huh?" She shook her head and laughed. "You go light a candle for that one Miles Montego."

"Love you, Ma."

"Love you too, baby."

Miles crossed the kitchen in two easy strides. "Tell Dad I said hello," he called over his shoulder. "And I'll holla at him later."

"Holla? What's 'holla,' Miles?"

Julia waited for her son's reply, but all she heard was his retreating footsteps followed by the sharp slam of the front door closing behind him.

2

"Look, y'all really need to tighten up your money game," Miles said, raising his voice slightly so he could be heard over the heavy, rhythmic bass reverberating in muffled pulses from the crowded nightclub just outside of the private lounge, where he had convened his boys. The dimly lit room with its polished concrete floors, leather paneled walls, and hanging plasma screens, was usually reserved for high-profile celebrities and their entourages. But Miles, who frequented the establishment several times a week and spent significant sums of money on premium cigars and top-shelf liquor every time he came in, had pull with one of the owners. On occasion, he reserved the secluded space so that he and his boys could relax away from the loud music and tangled mass of sweaty bodies on the main floor or, like tonight, so they could discuss business.

"Stop playing around and start thinking about your future, you feel me?" Leaning forward, Miles paused and met each one of the familiar faces seated around him with a meaningful look. These four guys weren't simply good friends; they weren't just his tight-knit inner circle. Miles trusted them wholly with the very same life he would give to protect them. They were his family. As close to him as any blood relative, these guys were his allies, his partners, his brothers.

As usual, Chris was the first to chime in. "Yo, Miles. What's there to think about?" he asked with a casual shrug. "We make money, then we spend it, then we make some more." The fellas laughed and despite himself, Miles joined them.

Chris was a natural-born hustler. When they were kids, he routinely enlisted Miles and the rest of the gang into helping him pull off his sometimes brilliant, sometimes half-baked, get-rich-quick schemes. More often than not, they made chump change by stealing packs of Newports from the corner store and selling them to their friends at half price. But on rare occasions, Chris' ideas would hit pay dirt. Like the summer he got a job working at the Shoe Palace in the local mall. When his manager was busy helping customers, Chris passed the flyest sneakers out the back door to Miles and the rest of the waiting crew, who would then sell them to the neighborhood kids for a fraction of what they were worth. They made a killing—enough to buy the cherry red Conion boom box, conspicuously displayed in the front window of Fry's Electronics—and became legends in their own minds.

Twenty years later Chris and the fellas had graduated from peddling the hottest kicks in their San Jose neighborhood to operating one of the largest drug rings in the state of California. And their game didn't stop at pills and powder. They'd built a reputation for themselves on the streets as the go-to guys for everything from guns to electronics.

"Y'all think this is a joke, but it ain't no game," Miles said, his jaw set. "I spend a lot of time looking at all the angles, covering up all my tracks so I don't get in no trouble."

From the corner of his eye, he saw Percy, forehead puckered with concentration, nod in a silent show of respect and admiration. A man of few words, P-Body rarely spoke at these meetings—or anywhere else for that matter—but he was always listening, always learning.

Standing six feet tall by the time he was fourteen, he'd been dubbed the crew's enforcer just by virtue of his size. Though he was a gentle guy, laid-back with a languid gait and a slow drawl to match, he was fiercely protective of everything and everyone he loved. The crew learned early on that if any one of their mouths wrote a check their fists couldn't cash, P-Body could be counted on to settle the debt.

"You don't think I get noticed?" Miles asked. He glanced across the circle at Taylor. The only white boy in the bunch, he was known around the block as Wikki—a nickname bestowed to him when they were kids in honor of the song "Jam on It," which he listened to, on repeat, for nearly an entire summer. A New York transplant, he became an instant member of the crew after he'd pulled a blade on two dudes bent on giving Chris a back-alley beat down for selling them a pair of busted speakers. Short and wiry, Wikki had strikingly blue eyes, a boisterous laugh and a slick, fast-talking manner that tended to get them into just as much trouble as it got them out of.

"A young brotha driving a $300,000 car, living in a million-dollar home and Mommy and Daddy ain't nowhere in sight?"

Wikki smirked. Percy and Chris chuckled.

Miles sat back. "Listen, why do you think I asked y'all to partner up with me on these shows I'm doing?"

Chris shrugged as though the answer was obvious. "To make bank."

"It's an opportunity. To invest in something legit. To make clean money." Miles shook his head. "Just do yourselves a favor and write a check once in a while," he said with laugh. "Use a credit card every now and then, ya feel me?"

"Yo, Miles. Say no more, man. We feel you." Martin placed a firm hand on Miles' shoulder and gave a cursory glance around the table. Chris, Percy, and Wikki nodded in agreement.

Martin and Miles went back a long way—further than any of the others guys—and had shared a special bond ever since middle school, when Martin's mom died unexpectedly in a car accident. His dad, who never quite recovered from the loss, spent his days glued to the recliner with a bottle of Southern Comfort and his nights picking cases for a small warehouse on the city's east side.

Left to fend for himself, Martin spent more and more time with Miles' family. He was a regular presence at the Montego dinner table and the unofficial occupant of their spare bedroom. He spent holidays with them, took trips with them and even accompanied them to mass on Sundays.

To their credit, Miles' parents never complained or asked any questions. They knew Martin's story, saw his need, and accepted him as their own. And although in recent years Miles and Martin had chosen very different paths in life, they were and would always be each other's closest friends and most trusted confidants. "We in it to win it," Martin assured him.

"Cool." Satisfied that he'd made his point, Miles clapped his hands together and stood. "Enough business for one night." He flashed a devilish grin and motioned toward the door behind him. "What do you say we head out there and do what we do?"

Almost instantly the mood in the room segued from serious to celebratory as Miles and the rest of the crew emerged from the private lounge. Drawing stares and pounds from strangers and acquaintances alike, they snaked their way through the packed club to the bar.

Miles flagged down the bartender and ordered the usual—a round of Louis XIII—while the fellas checked out a group of fine honeys bumping and grinding provocatively on the dance floor.

Chuckling, Miles shook his head and took in the scene around him. There were clusters of women in barely there dresses and sky high heels and cliques of young men all trying to outdo each other in different versions of the same designer threads. There were strobe lights and smoke machines and giant speakers strategically suspended from the club's steel-joist ceiling. There were bouncers—big and scowling and festooned in perfunctory head-to-toe black—standing post at every entrance and a deejay spinning the hottest new joints from his perch high above the crowd.

It was a typical Friday night—one Miles had lived a thousand times before with his boys. But as he watched them laugh and talk among themselves, he couldn't help but feel that something was changing. Hanging out, getting faded, macking girls—it was all getting tired, old. He didn't know what or why, but lately he longed for something different, something more.

"Here ya go, man." The bartender slid five drams of scotch his way. Miles peeled off a few bills from the wad of cash in his pocket and slipped him enough to cover the drinks and a generous tip, while Wikki, Chris, P-Body, and Martin all grabbed a drink.

"To being young," Wikki said, raising his beveled glass in a toast. "Paid," P-Body added, holding up his drink. Chris bit his lip at a petite blonde, who eyed him flirtatiously as she sauntered by. "And irresistible," he said, throwing up his scotch, while keeping an eye trained on her swaying hips.

Miles laughed. "All right, then. Here's to being young, paid, irresistible..."

"And untouchable," Martin said, raising his drink last.

"And untouchable," Miles echoed, nodding as they all clinked glasses and drank to their success.

3

Special Agent Terry Edgemond surveyed the briefing room full of suited detectives and uniformed beat cops talking among themselves. They were young, eager—some of the best the respected veteran had seen in his thirty years with San Jose's Drug Enforcement Administration. If they couldn't crack the Montego ring, it couldn't be done.

"All right. Listen up," he barked. The low murmur of idle chatter quickly dissipated into silence, as everyone's focus turned to their superior. "You've all been handpicked to help with this operation. As some of you may already know, the agency has spent a considerable amount of time and money compiling the evidence we need to put these guys away for a very long time." He signaled for the two lead detectives on the case to join him up front. "Agent McDaniel and Agent Harris have worked on this nonstop for the past several months. They're familiar with the ins and outs of this group—who they are, how they operate—and will be getting you up to speed on everything you need to know."

Jason McDaniel adjusted his tie, before flipping off the lights and taking his place next to the projector. A straight-laced former Marine with a nose for the truth and a passion for justice, he'd spent twelve grueling, albeit gratifying, years working as a homicide detective with the LAPD before accepting a position with the DEA. Back then, he thought the switch would mean less time in the field and more evenings at home with his wife and kids. But three years with the agency had taught him that the only difference between catching murderers and nailing kingpins was the nameplate.

"We believe strongly that the Montego crew is one of the biggest drug rings operating in this region, with ties to several other states," he said. The projector flickered to life and a surveillance video of Miles, Martin, Chris, Wikki, and P-Body milling on a street corner flashed onto the white screen.

"They're cocky, dangerous, and unfortunately for us, very smart," Agent Harris added. He shoved his hands in his trouser pockets and rolled back on his heels. "Their operation's tight, efficient, and they don't like anyone coming between them and their money."

"First up, Percy 'P-Body' Taylor." Wielding a small remote control, Agent McDaniel scrolled through a succession of still photos. "He's the muscle of this crew," he said, pausing on a close-up of P-Body in a do-rag and leather jacket. "And at 6'5" and 280 pounds, he's nothing to play with."

"Next up," Agent Harris continued. "We got Martin De LaFuente. He's the crew leader's best friend and right-hand man." P-Body's picture was replaced by one of Martin dressed in a black tee shirt and matching skull cap. A lit cigarette dangled from his pursed lips. "You can rest assured that wherever you see the leader, you will see Mr. De LaFuente not too far behind."

Agent McDaniel waited while several officers jotted down notes, before continuing. "Here, we have Taylor Delmonico." A still shot of a scrawny guy with a blue baseball cap pulled low flashed across the screen. In one hand, he held a cell phone to his ear; in the other, he gripped a nondescript duffle bag. "Better known as Wikki," Agent McDaniel added. A wave of laughter rippled through the room. Agent McDaniel nodded. "I know. I agree with you. He has a stupid name. But don't be fooled. He's their main runner, suspected of transporting large amounts of narcotics to Nevada, Arizona, and even parts of Mexico."

"That's Christopher Mayor," Agent Harris said, motioning toward surveillance footage of Chris as it danced across the screen. He was chubby with wide brown eyes and hunched shoulders. "Looks innocent enough, right? That's what we thought until we learned he's the number one moneymaker for these guys."

"And last, but certainly not least, we have Miles Montego—the kingpin," Agent McDaniel said with a slight sneer. "This guy lives in a house that's worth more than all our houses put together."

"One of his dozen cars is worth all our cars combined," added Agent Harris, folding his arms across his chest. "And he wears what we make in a year on his wrist."

"He's young. He's rich..." Agent McDaniel glanced at a still shot of Miles on the projection screen. Standing next to a black Bentley, he wore a sizeable diamond stud in each of his ears and a thick, gold chain around his neck. "He's not bad looking," Agent McDaniel conceded with a shrug. "But I wouldn't exactly want to marry him off to my daughter."

"We have reason to believe he is *the* biggest drug trafficker in all of Northern California," Agent Harris explained. "Which is exactly why we want to nail this guy."

"We're working around the clock on this one, people." Agent McDaniel powered down the projector and turned on the lights. "Each and every one of these miscreants is considered armed and very dangerous."

"We want them off our streets and in orange jumpsuits," Agent Harris said. "The sooner the better."

"Any questions?" Agent McDaniel glanced around the room. "Good." He closed his file notes and tucked them under his arm. "Then let's make it happen."

4

They have not deleveraged their debt and we're going in the same direction—a coma economy.

And, by the way, the debt's only gotten worse under the president, for sure. And, by the way, it's going higher. They're expecting 22 trillion in debt over the next eight years.

I gotta make my point here.

Go ahead. Make your final point; we're all ears.

The bottom line is that stocks right now based on expected earnings from research analysts across the street—we are 15 percent undervalued and we should be about 10 to 15 percent overvalued. So, I believe there's no bubble right now in terms of earnings expectations.

Well, what, did expected earnings look like in 2007 in the United States? What did they look like in 1989 in Japan? They look great...until they crash.

Miles tuned out the squawk box fodder playing softly from the large flat screen television hanging on the wall across from his desk. For years, he'd made a habit of TiVo-ing a week's worth of the show and then catching up every Saturday morning on the ever-changing state of the world's financial markets.

He took a sip of his coffee before signing his name on the check he'd just filled out and slipping it, along with the payment stub, into a stamped envelope. Placing it atop a stack of other mail ready to be sent out, he reached for the next invoice waiting to be paid, when his cell phone rang.

Miles smiled at the name that flashed across the screen and answered the call with a swipe of his thumb. "Nick! How you doing?"

"I'm hanging in there—doing good," answered his longtime friend and financial advisor. "Not as good as you, though. You've got to learn to leave a little bit of that cash around so the rest of us can make some."

Miles laughed. "Come on, now. If I did that, you'd be out of a job."

"True, true," Nick said. His baritone voice filtered through the receiver in raspy puffs. "So, listen. It's fourth of July weekend and I got a real great group of people coming over." In the background Miles heard trees bristling and the faint clinking of silverware. "I got steaks from Argentina. I got lobsters from Maine. All I need is you to come hang out so I don't feel like I only know old people."

Miles glanced down at the paperwork strewn across his desk. "You know what? I think I might take you up on that."

"So you'll come by?"

"Yeah," he said, checking his watch. "I'll probably shoot over there in about an hour."

"Great." Nick's tone was triumphant. "See you in a bit."

5

Nick Holston's home was a sprawling mansion in the über-swanky suburb of Saratoga. A total of 12 acres, a vineyard estate nestled in the scenic Mount Eden foothills, lush and boasting stately oak trees, a winding creek, and even the occasional family of deer.

The private gravel road crunched beneath Miles' tires as he navigated his Bentley through the open security gate and around the majestic spray fountain situated at the center of the circular driveway.

It had been quite some time since he'd visited Nick and his wife, Karen, at their home, and as he bounded up the set of shallow steps toward the glass double doors, he found himself looking forward to a relaxing afternoon catching up with his good friends. Miles rang the doorbell, and moments later a slim figure approached.

"Well, hello stranger!" Karen Holston greeted Miles with a warm smile and a welcoming hug. She was tall and blonde with delicate features that reminded Miles of a porcelain doll. "It's been a long time."

"Too long." He handed her a bottle of wine he'd brought from his personal cellar. "Thanks for having me."

She dismissed his formality with an elegant wave of her slender hand. "We're just glad you could make it on such short notice."

"You look beautiful as always."

Laughing, Karen leaned forward with a conspiratorial wink. "Thank God for Botox," she said, stepping aside so Miles could enter. He followed her down a long corridor lined with fine art, through the cavernous kitchen and out of a set of French doors to the meticulously manicured expanse of land behind the house. Dozens of guests mingled in small cliques at the umbrellaed tables, comfy lounges, and buffet stations laden with elaborate arrays of fruits and cheeses littered across the large veranda. A smooth rhythm and blues melody played in the background, while kids squealed and laughed as they splashed in the glistening pool beside the bar.

Standing post behind the built-in grill, Nick sipped a soda and chatted cordially with two older gentlemen, both dressed in polo shirts, khaki pants, and loafers. "Look what the cat dragged in," he called when he saw Miles. Excusing himself, he put down his tongs and made a beeline in his direction. Heavyset with a full head of gray hair and goatee to match, Nick looked unusually casual in a pair of navy shorts and a white polo. "You made it," he said, shaking Miles' hand and then drawing him in for a hug.

Miles laughed. "I told you I would."

"Now we got a party. Hey, everyone," Nick shouted to those milling nearby. "This is Miles. See?" He jabbed an elbow at one of his passing guests. "I told you I had cool friends."

"Get outta here," Miles said. "I'm trying to be like you when I get old."

"Old?" Nick raised a brow in feigned offense. "Who you calling old?"

"My bad, my bad. Mature," Miles amended.

Nick laughed. "Nah. Who am I kidding? Old sounds about right."

Miles surveyed the idyllic scene around him—the bright blue elderberry and bristling evergreens, the jovial guests and the tasteful decor, all framed by the rolling Santa Cruz mountain range. His eyes rested on Karen carrying on an animated conversation with a group of ladies beneath the gazebo. She threw her head back in a spontaneous burst of laughter and Miles smiled. "Well, if this is old age, I look forward to it."

Nick followed his line of sight. "So, who you here with?"

"Me?" Miles shifted uncomfortably beneath Nick's searching gaze. "I'm solo today."

"Solo? What happened to the girl you brought with you to our Christmas party last year? Sheila or Sandra..."

"Shonda?"

"That's it. She was a real sweetheart. What happened to her?"

"It just didn't pan out." He shrugged. "She wasn't for me, I guess."

"I hate to break it to you, kid. But you ain't getting any younger," Nick joked. "Don't you want to settle down, start a family?"

"I do. But it's hard to find the right one when you grind like I do, Nick."

"Well, just be careful not to let money run your life." Nick gestured toward a group of men seated around a nearby table, seemingly engrossed in an intense discussion. "Otherwise you might end up like those guys."

Miles took in their designer sport shirts and tailored pants. "They look like they're doing all right to me."

"I'm serious, Miles. Earlier I'm asking one of those guys to pass the chips and he wants to know what the market closed at yesterday." Nick shook his head. "I mean, come on. Get a life!"

Miles laughed.

"But I can't really talk. I used to be the same way," Nick confessed. "And it almost cost me my family."

Miles' smile faded. "What do you mean?"

"It got to the point where I was never home, and if I did manage to show up, I was distracted—constantly juggling a million different things. Karen was ready to throw in the towel. Said she was tired of living with a stranger and asked for a divorce."

"Nick, man, I'm sorry to hear that."

"Don't be. It was just the incentive I needed to get my priorities in order. She agreed to counseling, and I've started leaving work at the office. I also committed to going to church every Sunday as a family and one date night a week."

"I never figured you as the religious type," Miles said.

Nick tilted his head from side to side. "The word religious is kind of like the term 'margin call' in the stock market. We try to steer clear of it. I prefer to think of myself as a man of faith."

Miles glanced from Nick to Karen, still laughing with her friends. "Well, it's working—whatever you choose to call it. You guys seem happy."

Nick smiled. "We are. I mean, we're not perfect. Some days are rougher than others, but we're getting there."

"All right, everyone! Food is ready," Karen called. She stood and motioned everyone over to the gazebo. "Can we all gather round and have a word of prayer before we eat?"

Obediently, Miles and Nick gathered with the others. As they joined the growing circle, Miles was caught off guard by a strikingly attractive woman standing across from him. She looked familiar, though he couldn't recall where he'd seen her or who she was. Rapt, Miles watched as a warm breeze blew her wavy black hair into her eyes. She tucked the strand behind her ear before turning her attention to Karen who was addressing the crowd.

"First I'd like to thank everyone for coming to our home today. We're grateful to have such wonderful people in our lives. All of you mean so much to us and Nick and I are blessed to know you." Smiling, she paused for a moment to study the faces congregated around her. "Someone once told me that friends are kisses blown to us by angels. And that's exactly what you are—heaven sent. So thank you, again, for coming and thank you—"

"Honey, honey." Nick gently placed his hand on the small of her back. "This isn't the Oscars. We're all starving here."

Everyone laughed.

"Well, I was just about to thank my wonderful husband for putting this all together," she said, planting a kiss on his check. "But I guess I'll just skip right to the prayer." Karen bowed her head and closed her eyes. The rest of them followed suit.

"Dear Father, thank You for this glorious day," Karen said. "It's so easy to believe in You—to have faith in You when we're blessed with such wonderful weather and delicious food..."

Miles tried to resist the urge to sneak another peek at the gorgeous woman a few feet away, but curiosity got the better of him. He pried one eye open and studied her intently.

She was wearing a gauzy yellow cardigan over a white tee shirt and a pair of cutoff shorts that accentuated her long, toned legs. He took note of the small crucifix hanging from her neck and the matching gold studs decorating each earlobe. Brows furrowed, she listened attentively and every now and then nodded her head in agreement as Karen continued to pray, while Miles racked his memory trying to remember where he'd seen those pillowy lips and delicately pointed chin.

She definitely wasn't a business associate. And he was fairly certain they didn't meet at any of the nightclubs he frequented; if they had, he wouldn't have let her get away without learning her name or getting her number. A fleeting image of the mystery woman in the silver convertible from a few days earlier flashed across his mind.

It couldn't have been her. He dismissed the possibility with a shake of his head. What were the chances that he'd chased his dream girl all through downtown San Jose just to find her in his friend's backyard? Those sorts of against-the-odds coincidences didn't happen in real life, he reasoned. At least, not to him. Miles narrowed his eyes and took another good look at her. Or did they?

"That's Vanessa." Nick's voice startled Miles to attention. He'd been so lost in thought that he hadn't realized Karen finished praying or noticed that most of the guests circled around her had disbanded and had already begun to pile their plates high with food.

Miles shifted uncomfortably beneath the weight of Nick's searching gaze, embarrassed to have been caught staring, but relieved to finally know her name. "Vanessa, huh?"

"Yeah. She goes to Bible study every week with my wife." Grinning, Nick patted his shoulder. "Come on. I'll introduce you."

Miles followed Nick the few feet to where Vanessa was seated with Karen and a group of other ladies chatting and laughing over a bottle of wine. "Miles!" Karen's face lit up when she saw him. "Let me introduce you to some of my girlfriends," she said, waving him over.

Smiling, Miles nodded hello. "How y'all doing?"

"This is Shari," Karen said, pointing to the blond woman at the farthest end of the table. Shari waved. "Hi."

"That's Maylin," Karen continued. "That's Sarah."

Both women smiled.

"Nice to meet you," Maylin said.

Sarah nodded. "Pleasure."

"And this," Karen gestured to the woman next to her, "is Vanessa."

Vanessa smiled and revealed two perfect rows of pearly white teeth. "Hi. How are you?" she asked, extending her hand toward Miles.

He shook it. "Good. How are you?"

"I'm good." Their eyes locked and his heart began to beat a little faster. She was even more stunning up close and in person. "Miles is a very cool name."

"Thank you," he said, working to keep his tone even, casual. Though he was known among his friends for being something of a smooth-talking ladies' man, he found himself at a rare loss for words. Their polite chitchat quickly gave way to awkward silence.

Vanessa laughed. "Can I get my hand back before I call 911?"

Miles looked down at her palm still nestled against his. "I'm sorry," he said, releasing her hand. Instinctively, he took a step back.

Vanessa smiled, leaning forward to make up the space he'd put between them. "I was just teasing. It's cool."

Nick, who'd been silently watching their exchange along with the others, cleared his throat. "Well, I hope everyone's hungry. We've got a great spread and enough to feed an army. So, please, help yourselves."

"I think I saw a crab cake with my name on it," Sarah said as she, Shari, and Maylin pushed their chairs back from the table.

Vanessa also stood. She glanced up at Miles. "I'm starving. How about you?"

He nodded. "I could eat."

"Great." She in a grand sweeping gesture. "Shall we?"

"Most definitely," he said, leading the way to the closest buffet table. He handed her a plate, before taking one for himself.

Vanessa served herself a salmon steak and a few shoots of grilled asparagus. "So, how do you know the Holstons?" she asked.

"Well, you know, Nick's my broker and money guy." He shrugged. "So we hang out from time to time."

She paused, an expression of amusement and intrigue on her face. "So young and into stocks?"

"You're never too young to start making good investments," he said, smiling as he placed a couple of shrimp skewers on his plate. "So, how do you know Nick and Karen?"

"We actually all go the same church. And Karen and I are members of the same women's Bible study."

"I take it you're Christian, then."

She nodded. "I am, but we don't really like to call it that."

"Me either." Miles thought back to his conversation with Nick. "I prefer the term, man of faith." Thoughtfully, he tilted his head. "Or in your case, woman of faith."

"Exactly," she said, her eyes brimming with pleasant surprise. "So you know what I'm talking about."

He smiled. "Yeah, of course."

"What church do you go to?"

His smile faded. "Me? Oh…well, you know…I'm kind of in between churches at the moment."

"Okay." Vanessa's forehead puckered with suspicion. "Well, what was the name of the last church you attended?"

"God is Great…Holy Trinity…Peace and Blessings Tabernacle," he said, uneasily stringing together the limited bits of Christian terminology in his vocabulary.

She laughed. "You are so playing with me right now, Mr. Miles."

"Okay, okay. You caught me." Miles abandoned all pretense of piety. "Truth is, I was brought up Catholic, but...I don't know...I never stuck with it." He shrugged. "I guess I didn't really feel comfortable at my church."

Vanessa considered his words for a moment. Miles braced for her response, hoping that his candidness hadn't turned her off.

"Then you should find a church that you do feel comfortable at," she said, her tone sincere, encouraging. "And stick with it."

His eyes met hers and he smiled. "Thanks. Maybe I will."

Over lunch, they traded life stories. Miles told her about his close bond with his parents and shared many anecdotes, much to her amusement, about his crew and their mischief-making youth. He opened up about his desire to one day travel the world, to learn a new language, and to eventually settle down and give his mom her long-awaited grandkids.

Vanessa shared fond memories from her own childhood with her mom, dad, and two sisters. She described the events that influenced her decision to return to college and pursue a degree in special education and detailed the rigors that came with keeping on top of her studies and holding down a part-time job.

Miles found her fascinating and hung on to her every word with rapt interest. He memorized her mannerisms—the animated way she moved her hands when she talked about her love for children; the flush of excitement that traveled up her neck and colored her cheeks when she described her dream of one day making a difference in the lives of autistic kids.

With every new tidbit Vanessa shared, Miles wanted to know more about her. No detail was too small, no fact too insignificant. They talked and laughed for what seemed liked ages—long after their food had been eaten, their plates had been cleared, and the sun had dipped behind Mount Eden's gently rolling hills.

"Wow," Miles looked around at the nearly empty veranda, now dimly lit by beautifully strung pixie lights and paper lanterns. The last of the stragglers, they were reclined on adjacent loungers in front of a stone hearth, enjoying the heat from the quietly crackling fire. "I guess we shut this joint down, didn't we?"

"Looks like it," Vanessa said, glancing around. "I should probably go. It's getting late."

Miles felt a pang of disappointment as he watched her sit up and slide her feet into her sandals. "So, maybe we can see each other again—that is, if you can find time between school and saving the world."

"Please, Miles. My life is not that serious." Shaking her head, she laughed. "But, yes. I'd love to."

He smiled. "Cool. Let me see your phone."

She pulled it from her back pocket and handed it to him. "I have a good idea," she said, watching as he snapped a picture of himself and added his name and number to her contacts. "How about we not play the who-can-wait-the-longest-to-call-who game."

Miles laughed. "Yeah, I don't like that game either," he said returning her phone. "Okay, I got a better one. How about we play the who-can-call-who-first game instead?"

"Ahhh, see?" She smiled. "I'm into that."

He smiled back. "I'm into that too."

"Good." Their gazes met and a brief, meaningful silence settled over them. "It's definitely time for me to go," she said, standing.

"So, I'll talk to you soon?"

Vanessa stopped and looked back. Her lips curled up into a playful smile. "Not if I talk to you first." And with that she turned and disappeared into the night.

6

By six o'clock Sunday morning, Miles had already gone for a run, taken a shower, eaten breakfast, and answered several emails when he received a video message on his iPad.

Grabbing his coffee, he settled into his favorite armchair and pressed the message icon, expecting to watch the latest trading update from his investment broker in New York. Instead, he was greeted by a familiar smile.

He sat up, suddenly alert. "Good morning, Vanessa," he said, pressing play.

"Hello Mr. Miles," her recording began. She was lying in bed, fresh faced with her hair pulled into a messy bun on top of her head. "Look, I know it's a little early, but my Sundays usually start when the sun comes up. I just wanted to say that I really enjoyed meeting you yesterday and I look forward to, hopefully, hanging out with you again." She bit her lip. "Well, I guess that's it. Have blessed day, Mr. Miles Montego. Oh, and by the way, I win the game." Throwing up deuces, she giggled. "Peace."

Grinning, Miles grabbed his phone and dialed her number. She picked up on the first ring. "Well aren't we quite the busy bee at 6 a.m.?"

Vanessa's laugh was infectious and uninhibited. "You're awake?"

"Ain't no question." He switched the phone from one ear to the other. "My days usually start around 5 a.m. anyways."

"5 a.m.!" Her tone was one of disbelief. "What are you, a baker?"

He chuckled. "Nah, I deal a lot with the East Coast so the time difference gets me up."

"Okay, big shot." He heard the springs of her mattress creak beneath her shifting weight. "So, how about it, you want to come to church with me today?"

Miles paused, caught off guard by the invitation. "You know what...I got a gang of stuff to get done by tomorrow." Vanessa was quiet on the other end. "But I'll definitely take a rain check on that, if it's all right with you."

"Of course. Anytime," she said, her disappointment plain. "Listen, I've gotta run right now, but maybe we can talk later?"

"What do you say we leave the maybes out of this and just get together after we both do what we gotta do?"

Vanessa's voice, sweet and smiling, danced against his ear, "I say, that sounds like a plan to me."

7

"Miles, this place is beautiful!" Vanessa exclaimed. Her eyes, wide with surprise, traveled the length of his marble foyer. Appointed with vaulted ceilings and an ornate chandelier, it opened up to a circular gallery flanked by a pair of heirloom staircases that curved upward toward the home's second floor.

"Thank you," he said, smiling as she took a few cautious steps forward and peeked around the corner into the formal dining room he rarely used.

"You live here all by yourself?"

Miles shrugged. "Unless there are some roaches I don't know about."

"But it's so big," she marveled, mostly to herself. She turned to look at him. "How many bedrooms are there?"

"Last time I checked…eight."

"Eight bedrooms for one person!" Her voice echoed off the gilded walls.

"What can I tell you?" He deadpanned. "I needed the extra closet space."

Vanessa laughed. "*No one* should have that many clothes," she said, playfully wagging of her finger.

"I know, I know. I'm just messing with you." He looked around the space he called home, with its custom furnishings and high-end appointments and sighed. "I guess the truth is I bought this place in preparation for the life I hope to have someday."

"And what life is that?" she asked.

"You know, the whole family thing." Miles looked away, feeling suddenly shy. "Wife, kids, dog…maybe a goldfish or two." He laughed at himself. "Sounds kind of crazy when I say it out loud."

"It's not crazy." Vanessa's gaze was kind. "You've got a dream; there's nothing wrong with that. Some of the greatest men who ever lived were the ones courageous enough to dream."

He took a moment to consider her words. "Thanks, I never thought of it that way."

"Well, you should." She smiled. "And don't give up on that life you want. In my experience, 'someday' is never quite as far away as you think."

"I hope you're right," he said, grinning, as she was, at the inescapable possibility that their someday was starting now.

~

"Chateau d'Yquem's Sauternes 2008," the sommelier announced, expertly displaying the bottle of wine Miles had selected, then pouring a small amount into each of their glasses in one deft movement.

"Thank you." Vanessa nodded her appreciation.

"My pleasure." He nestled the bottle in a small ice bucket, before excusing himself with a small, gracious bow.

"I still can't believe you reserved the entire terrace," Vanessa said, glancing around the secluded area from their candlelit table.

"It was no trouble, really. The owner's a good friend." Miles smiled. "I just wanted our first date to be special. You know, something to remember."

She laughed. "Well, mission accomplished. This is definitely not an evening I will ever forget."

He gestured at the menu in her hand. "Do you know what you're gonna order?"

"I can't decide." Her eyes skimmed the list of delicacies for what felt like the hundredth time. "Everything looks so good." She noticed his menu, resting unopened by his place setting. "What are you having?"

"The braised lamb," he said. "They serve it with a cherry bordelaise that'll make your toes curl."

She shook her head and leaned forward. "A cherry what?"

He chuckled. "It's like a red wine sauce."

Vanessa smiled, as impressed as she was curious. "Who are you?" she asked, studying him appraisingly. "What's your secret?"

He tilted his head. "What do you mean?"

"Like, did the stock market get you all of this—the house, the cars, the connections?" She motioned around the private terrace. "Or did you run into some amazing family fortune?"

"There's no secret," he said, grinning. "I work hard and I like to keep my hands in a lot of different things. Like, right now, I have a string of concerts I'm doing."

"Where, here in the Bay?"

"Yeah. I got one in Frisco, one in Oakland and one right here in San Jose."

"Wow, Miles. That's exciting."

"You know, I was thinking...maybe, you might wanna come hang out with me for a couple of the shows? You don't gotta go to all of them, but, you know..." His sentence trailed off and he shrugged. "It should be a good time."

Narrowing her eyes, Vanessa raised a brow. "Mr. Miles, are you asking me on another date?"

He watched as the glow from the flickering candles formed a warm halo around her bare shoulders. An automatic smile crept across his face. "I guess I am."

"Well—" Her answer was cut short by Miles' ringing cell phone.

Miles glanced at the number. "Oh, man," he said, his tone apologetic. "I gotta take this one. I'm sorry."

"Don't be." She shooed him off. "I understand."

"I'll be right back."

Miles quickly made his way through the crowded dining room and onto the quiet sidewalk just outside the restaurant's main entrance.

~

"Yo."

"What's buzzin cuzzin?"

"T, what's going on, man? What's happening?"

From their surveillance van parked a few yards down the block, Agent McDaniel and Agent Stokes listened closely to Miles' phone call.

"You know, just trying to make a dollar out of 15 cents," T said with a chuckle. "Hey, did you fire off that package yet?"

"Sure thing. It'll be on your desk by tomorrow morning. Probably around ten o'clock."

McDaniel and Stokes watched through a video feed as Miles paced a few steps forward, then doubled back the way he came.

"Man, I like your style Miles," T said. "So you're all locked and loaded on your end, right?"

"Oh yeah, man. For sure. Everything's set up just the way we planned. So I'll see y'all in a couple weeks."

"All right. One love, baby."

McDaniel removed his headphones as the call terminated and Miles went back into the restaurant. "What've we got on this T character?" he asked.

Stokes shook his head. "Not much. The number traces to a cell phone outside of Ohio. My best guess is he's a client or a connection—possibly another trafficker."

"I think you might be right," McDaniel said. "Call Harris. Tell him we got a possible lead and see if he can cross reference the number against our database. Maybe we'll get lucky. In the meantime, I want the team to dig up everything they can on this guy...names of family members, friends, phone records, bank statements, last known addresses, criminal history— the works. If he so much as sneezed in the past six months, I want to know about it."

"I'm on it," Stokes said, already dialing headquarters.

McDaniel returned his attention to the monitor in front of him. Leaning forward, he rewound the footage of Miles and played it back in slow motion.

"I'm coming for you, Montego," he whispered, pausing the video on a grainy frame of Miles looking over his shoulder. "Mark my words: your days are numbered."

~

"Sorry about that," Miles said, reclaiming his seat across from Vanessa.

"No problem. Is everything okay?"

"Yeah, everything's cool."

"You sure?" She looked unconvinced as she nibbled her bottom lip. "I mean, if you need to rain check or something, I would completely understand."

"No, no, no, not at all. Matter of fact," he said, reaching for his phone. "Let me turn this off right now so we can enjoy ourselves without any more interruptions."

"No," Vanessa placed her hand over his. "Don't you dare, Miles."

"Really, it's okay." His smile was reassuring. "Whatever it is can wait until after dinner."

"Please don't." She tightened her grip around his hand. "Like, it's clearly business. I would never ask you to do that."

"You know what? That's dope," he said, an unmistakable lilt of admiration in his voice. "A lot of women would get an attitude, you know, accuse me of being rude or whatever."

She shrugged. "I guess I'm not most women."

"No. You're not." He flipped his hand so that his palm was pressed against hers and intertwined their fingers. "Now, where were we?"

She looked up, feigning deep thought. "I believe you had just finished asking me on a second date."

"Right." Gently, he caressed the soft curve of her knuckles with his thumb. "So, what do you think?"

Propping her elbow on the table, she rested her chin in her hand and leaned forward with a smile. "I'd love to."

The rest of the evening flew by in a satiating haze of good food, great conversation, and nonstop laughter. Alone in the night on the dimly lit terrace, they were lost in their own world—one devoid of time, worries, and awareness of anything or anyone besides each other. By the time they left, the main dining room had long been cleared of the last patrons and the cleaning team, which had replaced the wait staff, was fastidiously placing the chairs upside down on the tables.

Miles's disappointment was palpable as he pulled into his driveway and he and Vanessa strolled, hand in hand to her car.

"I had a really good time," she said. "And I'm not just saying that."

"Me too." He paused at the sight of her Sebring and smiled. "You drive a silver convertible."

She looked from Miles to her car to Miles again. "Yeah, so?"

He laughed. "So you wanna hear a funny story?"

"Sure," she said, her expression one of bewilderment.

"A few weeks ago, I'm driving, when I come to a stop sign and I see this convertible," he said, inching closer. "But what really caught my eye was this beautiful woman behind the wheel."

Involuntarily, Vanessa's body leaned forward.

"She had this long, beautiful hair," he said, twirling one of her glossy locks around his finger. "Kind of like yours. And she was wearing these shades—these really hot shades. I felt like I had to catch her. I mean, I was on her. I'm holding up traffic, bobbing and weaving in between cars." Smiling, Miles glanced away. "Make a long story short, I get pulled over by a cop and she slips away. But you know what really bothered me?"

Vanessa shook her head as Miles snaked his arm around her waist and pulled her to him.

"I didn't get a chance to meet her, to know who she was."

"What kind of car did you say she was driving?" Her words came out as a whisper.

Miles delicately grazed his thumb along her cheek and down the contour of her jaw before hooking it beneath her chin and tilting her face toward his. "A silver convertible Sebring," he said, slowly lowering his lips to hers and ending the perfect night with the perfect kiss.

8

Vanessa used a box cutter to slice through the packing tape of another new shipment of merchandise. She picked up one of the books inside and passed it to her co-worker, Kristi. By rote, Kristi scanned the book into the store's inventory system and then handed it off to a second co-worker, Heather, who tagged it with a pricing gun and loaded it onto a cart of items waiting to be shelved. Plugging away at their work, they operated like a well-oiled production line—rhythmically passing, scanning, and tagging—as customers browsed the sales floor.

But as Kristi and Heather cheerfully chatted about nothing and everything under the sun, Vanessa found her thoughts drifting back to Miles. She'd replayed the date in her mind on a continuous loop and, still, the memory of their time together made her pulse quicken and her head light. It had been like something out of a fairytale—from the romantic setting and the private table to the amazing food and stimulating conversation. And then, there was the kiss.

An involuntary smile spread across her lips. She could still feel the soft press of his mouth against hers, still smell the intoxicating scent of his cologne and hear the deep rumble of his voice as he said goodnight.

Part of her knew it was crazy. How could she be falling so hard, so fast for a guy she barely knew? At first she'd chided herself for being so recklessly free with her heart. What if he wasn't who he portrayed himself to be? What if he was just like so many of the others who'd come before him—a slick talker looking for a cheap fling and an easy target? The potential for getting hurt was very real and it scared her. But then she envisioned his face, with his lazy smile and come-to-bed eyes, and all of her doubts—every last one of her reservations—vanished.

Vanessa handed Kristi the last book in the shipment, then swiftly broke down the empty box and tossed it on top of the slowly amassing pile of flattened cardboard in the corner, when a figure in the distance caught her attention. She froze.

"Oh my gosh, oh my gosh!" she said, hiding her smile beneath her trembling hand. She turned away and faced the wall behind the checkout counter. Instantly, her stomach churned with an unsettling mixture of nervousness and excitement.

Dropping her scanner, Kristi rushed to her side. "What's wrong?"

"He's here," Vanessa hissed. She rubbed her clammy palms against her pant legs.

"Who's here?" Heather abandoned her post behind the register, and quickly joined the huddle.

"Him," Vanessa whispered. Unable to muster enough nerve to turn around, she nodded her head in the general direction of the door.

Heather's green eyes widened as her expression morphed from confusion to curiosity. "Miles?"

"Where, which one is he?" Kristi asked, searching the store full of customers.

Vanessa hushed them. "Don't say his name so loudly." She glanced over her shoulder. "He might hear you."

Her heart thudded loudly against her chest as she watched him casually peruse a rack of clearance items at the front of the store. He looked undeniably handsome dressed in a grey cashmere hoodie and cuffed dark-wash jeans.

"Is that him?" Kristi and Heather followed her gaze.

"Girl, he is *fine!"* Heather said.

"I know, right?" she asked, smiling as he made his way from the clearance rack to a display of key chains and decals.

Nodding, Kristi took him in from head to toe. "I so hate you right now."

"Well don't just stand there," Heather prodded, gently shoving Vanessa forward. She smirked. "We all know he's not here to buy a Jesus bumper sticker for his Bentley."

Vanessa combed her fingers through her hair and smoothed the nonexistent wrinkles from her blouse as she walked toward him.

"Hey, you," he said, his face brightening the minute he saw her. He bent forward and gave her a peck on the cheek.

She felt her face flush. "Hey. What are you doing here?"

"I was in the neighborhood, so I thought I'd stop by." He gave her a questioning look. "I hope that's okay."

"Of course it is," she said, smiling. "This is a nice surprise."

Miles glanced around at the colorful posters on the wall, the racks of graphic tees, the aisles of books and music and display cases of jewelry and other trendy accessories. "I love the spot. What kind of store is this?"

"Thanks. We're a faith-based products store," she said, leading him on an informal tour. "We carry Christ-themed gear, books, movies, CDs... things like that."

He looked skeptical. "Is there a big market for this church stuff?"

"Huge," she said.

Miles took a detour through the music section. "Are these all Christian artists?"

Vanessa nodded. "We got a little bit of everything—pop, R & B, Gospel..."

"Yo, this dude, right here, looks like a real rapper," Miles said, picking up a T-Bone CD.

"Come on, Miles." Vanessa watched as he thoughtfully thumbed through the album artwork. "He *is* a real rapper. He just raps about the Lord."

"I didn't mean it like that. I'm just saying, look." He flipped back to the cover and showed Vanessa the photo of T-Bone scowling, his hair slicked back into a braided ponytail. "This dude looks like a real gangsta."

Vanessa placed a hand on her jutted hip. "Are you telling me you've never listened to Christian music before?"

"Nah." Miles returned the CD to its shelf. "Well, my mom used to play her Elvis Presley Gospel albums on Sundays, if that counts."

"No, definitely not." Vanessa shook her head with a laugh. "You know what? It's your lucky day, cause I'm 'bout to hook you up. Don't go anywhere."

"I wouldn't think of it," Miles said, grinning as she dashed away. He ambled through the movie aisles and then the book section before making his way back to the front of the store where Vanessa was behind the register bagging CDs.

"So what you got for me?"

"I'm not even gonna tell you," Vanessa said. "Just trust me. It's hot." She smiled. "Promise me you'll listen?"

"Scout's honor," Miles pledged. "So, how much do I owe you?"

She slid the bag his way and shrugged. "Consider it a gift from me to you."

"That's what's up." He smiled. "So listen, I've got this birthday party I'm going to tonight and I thought maybe you'd wanna come with me. If you're free, that is."

"Yeah, I think I'd be able to swing that."

"Cool. How does seven o'clock sound?"

"Sounds good," she said. "You can pick me up at my place. Meet the family."

"Meet the family?" Smirking, he arched an eyebrow. "Uh-oh, this is getting serious."

"They're harmless. You'll be fine." She paused and tilted her head musingly. "Just steer clear of the coat closet; it's where my dad keeps his shotgun."

"Ah, see? You got jokes." He pointed an accusatory finger at her from across the counter. "Keep messing around and a brotha just might show up to your house in a helmet and a bullet-proof vest."

Vanessa erupted into laughter.

"See you at seven," Miles said, backing away with a smile.

"See you then." Watching as he headed toward the exit, Vanessa, Kristi, and Heather waited for Miles to cross the store and disappear into the crowd outside before bursting into an ear-piercing cacophony of excited squeals.

9

Obeying the navigation system built into his dashboard, Miles decelerated and smoothly maneuvered his Bentley onto a quaint street lined with manicured bushes and colorful craftsman-style bungalows. Drawing closer to Vanessa's house, he become increasingly aware of the metrical thuds of his rapidly pounding heart.

Generally, he was a confident guy—cool, calm, and collected in even the most challenging situations. In his line of work, he'd rubbed elbows with famous actors and professional athletes, best-selling authors, and award-winning musicians, but none of them had ever turned his insides in knots the way Vanessa did.

She was every man's fantasy—gorgeous and easy-going with a sharp wit and a level head. And she was sexy, not just because of the way she looked, but because she could talk cars and sports as easily as she could fill out a dress and strut around in heels. She was a church girl who went to Bible study and could spout Scriptures at the drop of a dime. Yet she never preached or judged or tried to change who he was. Her ready acceptance of him had been without questions or conditions. And that, he realized, as he pulled into her driveway and put his car into park, was why he was falling in love with her.

Miles checked his reflection in the rearview mirror, before exiting his car and trailing the walkway across the front yard. Bounding up the porch steps, he took a long, deep breath before ringing the bell.

"Is someone gonna get that?" he heard a muffled female voice shout from inside the house. The sound of heavy footsteps grew louder as the person neared and unlocked the deadbolt.

A teenage girl appeared on the other side of the screen door. She had Vanessa's high cheekbones and warm brown eyes. She also had the same glossy black hair, but worn in a short bob with a side-swept bang. At the sight of Miles, her irritated scowl turned into a coy grin. "Have mercy," she said, taking him in from head to toe with one approving glance.

Miles smiled. "Hi."

"I'll call you back," she said into the cordless phone pressed against her ear. She hung up with the press of a button and stepped aside so Miles could enter. "Hi." Her tone was flirtatious, hopeful. "I'm Alyssa."

"I'm Miles," he said, shaking her hand. "I'm here to pick up Vanessa."

"Figures." Alyssa rolled her eyes, her sweet demeanor gone just as quickly as it came. "Vanessa!" Her sharp voice rang through the small house. "Somebody's here for you!"

No sooner had she stomped down the hall and out of sight than he saw another young lady—also eerily similar in appearance to Vanessa—distractedly digging beneath the couch cushions and rummaging through the coffee table drawer. "Mom! Have you seen my car charger?" She shouted with such force that Miles was sure he saw the windows rattle. "I can't find it anywh—" Her words cut off midsentence when she spotted Miles standing by the front door. She smiled. "You must be Vanessa's date. I'm her younger sister, Julissa."

Miles pressed a hand to one of his ears in an attempt to stop it from ringing. "Does everyone yell around here?" he asked. "Because y'all are killing me right about now."

Julissa laughed. "Yeah, we're pretty much loud as can be. Don't worry though," she said, leaning forward with a conspiratorial wink. "You get used to it. Anyway, it was nice meeting you."

He opened his mouth to tell her the same, but she slipped away before he could respond. He chuckled. Suddenly it was very clear where Vanessa had acquired her lively candor and trademark spunk.

A stout gentleman with slight jowls and peppered hair emerged from the same hallway down which Julissa had just disappeared. He studied

Miles appraisingly, before offering him a firm handshake. "I'm Miguel Leon and you are?"

"Miles Montego," Miles said, instinctively standing more erect.

"Wow, Miles Montego. Sounds like a secret agent name." Miguel smiled. "Man of mystery."

Miles shook his head. "Sorry to disappoint, but there's no mystery here." He shrugged. "What you see is what you get."

"Even better," Miguel said, hooking an arm around Miles' shoulders and leading him into the nearby living room. "I'll take an honest man over a mysterious one any day. Have a seat." He motioned toward the sofa. "Can I get you anything—water, iced tea?"

"No. Thank you, I'm fine."

"Well, Vanessa should be down shortly." Miguel started to lower himself into the armchair across from Miles, but stood abruptly when an older woman entered the room. She was slender with deep-set eyes framed by faint crow's feet and skin that looked olive beneath her white ruffled cardigan. Her expression was stern as she glanced curiously from Miles to Miguel and back to Miles.

"Lydia," Miguel said, motioning her closer. "Honey, this is Vanessa's date."

Her disapproval of him was plain.

"Nice to meet you, Mrs. Leon," Miles said, standing to greet her. He extended his hand.

She didn't take it. "You're Miles?"

"Last time I checked," he said with a nervous chuckle.

Her grin was guarded. "And what is it that you do?"

"Well, I like to keep my hands in a little bit of everything," he said.

She pursed her lips. "That sounds promising. And how long have you been doing a little bit of everything," she asked, sounding skeptical and bored at the same time.

Miles shifted uncomfortably beneath her demanding stare. "Oh, well, you know..." There was no good answer to her question.

She folded her arms across her chest. "What church do you attend?"

"Oh, it's um…" His mind drew a blank. "I can never remember the name." He shrugged helplessly. "I just started going there."

"Really." Her eyes narrowed suspiciously.

"Honey," Miguel said, jumping to his rescue. "He's Vanessa's date, not a Russian spy. Enough with the interrogation."

"I want to know who my child is hanging out with," she said, her tone unapologetic. "Is that so wrong?"

"There's plenty of time for that," Miguel said soothingly. "I've got a feeling we'll be seeing a lot more of Miles."

The look on Lydia's face was one of unmistakable disappointment.

Miles was at a loss. Most moms loved him, but Lydia Leon seemed wholly unimpressed by everything about him. Feeling awkward and out of place, his gaze bounced from the floor to the ceiling to the neat collage of family photos hanging on the wall beside him. He looked anywhere, but the direction from which Mrs. Leon's searing stare was burning a hole into his forehead.

After several minutes of silence, he'd suffered all the discomfort he could bear and was about to offer to wait for Vanessa outside, when she descended the stairs in a form-hugging strapless dress that took Miles' breath away.

"I'm sorry I kept you waiting." She grabbed a sparkly blazer from the coat rack and slipped it on.

"Don't be," he said. Her mother's relentless questioning of him seemed suddenly inconsequential. "It was definitely worth it."

"Thank you!" She smiled.

"You ready to go?"

Vanessa nodded.

"Don't worry, Mrs. Leon," Miles said in a last-ditch effort to win over Vanessa's mother. "Your daughter's in good hands."

Lydia Leon gave him an icy once-over, then turned to Vanessa. "Don't stay out too late," she said, punctuating her order with a sharp nod.

And with that, she tossed her hair over her shoulder and exited the room without offering Miles so much as goodbye.

10

"No way! Can it be?" Chris asked, stooping to peer through Miles' tinted windows as he double-parked in front of the valet stand and exited his car. "Is that Miles Montego?"

Miles laughed. "The one and only, baby," he said, slapping hands with each member of the crew. "What's happenin' fellas? How you been?"

"Good, brother," Percy said. "Where you been hiding?"

Wikki shook his head. "Dogg, we thought you left the country or something."

"Nah, man." Miles brushed off the idea with a wave. "Just been busy, you know."

"Well, you lucky you showed up tonight," Martin said, pulling him in for a hug. "Cuz I was gonna go straight to your house from here, homie."

"Man, I wouldn't have missed this for nothing." Turning, Miles reached for Vanessa's hand and gently tugged her forward. "Fellas, I want to introduce you to my new lady, here. This is Vanessa. Baby, this is Martin, Chris, Percy, and Wikki."

Eyebrows raised, Wikki's gaze trailed the length of Vanessa's curvaceous body. "Yo, dogg, at least now we know what you been busy doing," he said, jokingly punching Percy's arm.

Vanessa smiled. "Hey guys. It's nice to finally meet you. Miles talks about you all the time."

"Nice to meet you too, ma." Martin shook her hand. "Glad you could come hang. You know, celebrate with us."

"Speaking of celebrating," Chris said. "Let's go inside and get some drinks."

Martin grinned. "That's what I'm talking about. Time to get this party started!"

They headed toward the entrance, where they were met by a burly guard dressed all in black. He carried a walkie-talkie and an intimidating scowl. Vanessa looked at the roped-off entrance behind him, then at the long line of anxious clubbers waiting to get in. As they drew closer, the bouncer's many tattoos and bulging muscles came into sight. Vanessa gripped Miles' hand more tightly, certain that they were headed for trouble, but when the man saw them approaching, his austere expression lifted.

"Miles!" he bellowed, smiling as they bumped fists.

"Bootz, man, what's going on?"

"Not much. We been missing you around here, I'll tell you that much." He unhooked the rope blocking the door and stepped aside. "Go on in, man," he said, nodding hello to the rest of the crew as they entered.

Inside, the club, humid from the heat of all the bodies, smelled of booze and sweat. Vanessa followed Miles, easing her way around cliques of people—some milling, others dancing—past the bar and up a flight of stairs that led to an elevated lounge out of the way of the general crowd. Several cocktail waitresses bustled about, dropping off orders and taking new ones.

Walking ahead of them, the guys joined a group of women already seated on a couple of the velvet sofas stationed across the loft. "Ha, ha!" Miles clapped his hands together. "The gang's all here. Let me introduce you to the ladies, baby," he said, resting his hand against the small of her back. But just before they reached the table, someone called his name.

Miles turned. "Ay, Jerry! What's going on, man?"

Vanessa froze, stunned to see Jerry Rice, famed wide receiver and arguably *the* greatest player in NFL history, standing just a few feet away. A sports fanatic and diehard football fan, she'd followed his career from San Francisco to Oakland and even Seattle. In fact, one of her fondest memories as a kid was watching Super Bowl XXIX with her dad. Jerry scored three touchdowns and made ten receptions for 149 yards, clinching the win against the San Diego Chargers and forever cementing his superstar status in the Leon household.

"You're Hall of Faming it this year, aren't you?" Miles asked.

Jerry's smile was smug. "Hey, well, you know how we do it."

"Definitely, definitely." Miles nodded. "Congratulations. Really, man, it's a huge accomplishment."

"Thanks, Miles."

"Hey, Jerry, I want you to meet my girl," he said, gesturing toward Vanessa. "Baby, this is Jerry Rice. He's one of the greatest—"

"Babe, I know who Jerry Rice is."

"Excuse me." Miles put his hands up and took as step back.

Vanessa laughed. "It's pleasure to meet you, Mr. Rice," she said, hardly able to contain her excitement. "I'm a big, big fan."

"Thank you. The pleasure's all mine." He shook her hand. "And, please, call me Jerry."

"Yo, Jerry. You in a hurry?" Miles asked. "Or can I buy you a drink?"

Jerry shook his head. "Actually, man, I'm on my way out. But, listen, before I go, you still got me on those tickets for that show we talked about, right?"

"Jerry, c'mon, baby. Of course I got you."

"Thanks, man." He shook hands with Miles and pulled him in for a quick embrace. "I really appreciate it."

Miles gave him a pat on the back before pulling away. "Don't mention it."

Jerry turned to Vanessa. "You keep an eye on this guy right here. Make sure he stays in line," he said, giving her a genteel peck on the back of her hand.

She smiled. "Will do."

"All right. You two enjoy the rest of your night."

"Yeah, man. You do the same," Miles said, as Jerry made his way down the stairs and disappeared into the crowd.

"Oh my gosh, babe, I can't believe you're friends with him!" she squealed.

He nodded. "Yeah, he's a good dude."

"Babe, my dad is gonna trip when he finds out I met Jerry Rice!"

Miles laughed. "Well now that I know you're such big fans, next time I run into Jerry, I'll be sure to get you both his autograph."

"That's what's up," she said. Accepting his proffered arm, Vanessa allowed him to escort her to where the guys and their dates were seated, chatting animatedly among one another.

"Sorry for the hold up. I had to handle a little bit of business," he said, helping Vanessa out of her blazer. They settled onto one of the empty tufted benches. "Ladies, this is my baby, Vanessa."

"Great to meet you all," Vanessa said, after another round of introductions.

"Hey, so what's good, chico?" Martin punched Miles in the arm. "Let's order some shots."

"Nah, man. Imma have to pass," Miles said. "I'm driving."

Martin balked. "Not tonight, homie. It's my birthday, man. We celebrating."

Miles glanced over at Vanessa. She was leaning up against him smiling and nodding encouragingly.

Ordinarily, he wouldn't have hesitated to throw back a few drinks, but he knew how wild his boys could get when the liquor started flowing and he didn't want to subject Vanessa to that sort of crass behavior. It's not that she was uptight—one of those overly religious folks who thought drinking was a sin. But she was a different breed of woman than he was used to dating. Classy, respectable, and God-fearing, Vanessa raised the bar, not just for the way he thought or how he comported himself, but for the person he wanted to be.

"C'mon, man," Martin prodded. "I mean at least have one with us."

Miles relented with a shrug. "Maybe later."

"Yeah, all right." Martin waved off Miles' attempt at decorum. "Look, don't let the cuffs and collar fool you," he said to Vanessa. "Back in the day, I seen ya boy guzzle a fifth of Bacardi and still hold his own with a cat twice his size. Bam! Bam! Bam!" Martin threw two jabs and an uppercut. "Dropped him like it wasn't nothing."

"Or what about that time he was hanging out the window, guns blazing like a mad man," Chris said, nudging Percy with a laugh.

Percy held his arms out, index fingers curved as though they were squeezing a trigger. "My man was like, Prrah, Prrah, Prrah," Percy said, mimicking the sound of a machine gun. "It was crazy."

Vanessa sat up straight and looked at Miles, her forehead wrinkled with concern. He'd never mentioned any sort of wild past—certainly not one marked by drunken brawls and automatic weapons. The Miles she knew was a smart ingenious businessman with a big heart and even bigger dreams. She couldn't help but wonder what else he'd conveniently forgotten to mention, how much more he was hiding.

"I'm telling you, ma. That man right there…" Martin pointed at Miles. "You're sitting with a real legend."

"You know what?" Miles stood abruptly. "I think I'll take that shot after all. Let's go, fellas," he said, motioning for Martin, Chris, Percy, and Wikki to follow. "First round's on me."

Vanessa watched, at a loss for words, as the guys headed toward the bar.

"So, Vanessa," Nicole, Chris' girlfriend called from her perch on an adjacent sofa. "How did you and Miles meet?"

"Oh, um…" Vanessa shook her head, still distracted by what had just happened. "We met through mutual friends—the Holston's," she added, on the off chance she knew them too.

Martin's date, Simone—a waif of a woman with strikingly long legs and tight ringlets eyed her questioningly. "And how long have you two…" she let her sentence trail, clearly unsure how to define their relationship.

"Not long." Vanessa smiled. "But long enough for me to know he's a really special guy."

Smirking, Simone leaned forward. "So then it's true what they say about him."

"About what?" Vanessa asked.

"You know." Simone bounced her eyebrows suggestively.

Percy's girlfriend, Shaunice, grinned amusedly. "His performance."

Vanessa looked around the circle of women eagerly awaiting an answer to a question she honestly didn't understand. She shook her head, bewildered.

Jasmine, Wikki's girlfriend, laughed. "In the bedroom?"

"Oh, wow!" Vanessa sat back, literally bowled over by their brazen presumption. "Look, I'm not trying to keep you girls in suspense or anything, but I wouldn't know."

Simone balked. "You mean you guys haven't slept together yet?"

"We're just trying to take things nice and slow," she said, masking her annoyance with a cavalier shrug.

"Nice and slow?" Shaunice pursed her lips, skeptical.

"Seriously." Jasmine narrowed her eyes. "Are we talking about the same Miles?"

Vanessa shifted awkwardly in her seat as they erupted into laughter. Within moments, the foursome had moved on to another equally asinine topic, but her discomfort lingered. She'd thought meeting Miles' friends would be fun—another exciting step toward getting to know the amazing man who'd so unexpectedly shown up in her life and taken residence in her heart. It never dawned on her that she might not like what she learned. Or worse, that he might be someone totally different from the person he claimed to be.

When Miles returned with the guys, his stiff body language and evasive gaze belied his calm voice and casual smile. At the bar, he'd immediately ripped into them for getting out of pocket in front of Vanessa and had demanded that they tighten up. He'd wanted to reveal certain things about himself in his own time—preferably, later down the line, when he knew Vanessa's feelings for him were as strong as his were for her and he was more confident that his checkered past wouldn't scare her off. But his friends had unwittingly tipped his hand. And he would have to take his chances and hope that she could recognize the difference between the man he was now and the man he used to be.

The evening wore on and Martin, Chris, Wikki, and Percy remained on their best behavior. Everyone traded stories, joked, laughed, and danced. And, in time, the uneasy silence between Miles and Vanessa eased into a temporary, unspoken truce. But as the celebration wound to a close and they all said their goodbyes, Miles found himself growing increasingly anxious at the prospect of what was ahead.

The mood on the ride back to Vanessa's house was quiet and heavy—a suffocating miasma of unasked questions and tacit emotion. Miles's mind spun with a million thoughts, none of which he could put into words. Despite an earnest desire to initiate a dialogue about everything she'd heard, he stared ahead and wordlessly watched the waxing and waning headlights of the passing cars.

"Wow. That was quite an evening," Vanessa said, finally breaking the silence.

Miles tightened his grip around the steering wheel. "Yeah, it was."

"Don't you think we should talk about it?" Her tone was gentle, searching.

"I don't know what to say, babe. Other than, I'm sorry. I really thought they would have acted way cooler than that."

She leaned back against the headrest and sighed. "Honestly, it's not them that worry me, it's you."

"Look, everybody has a past, V—including me." Frowning, he looked away. "And I'm not particularly proud of some of the things I've done."

"We all have pasts, Miles."

"Yeah, but I feel like once you hear about mine, you won't want to see me no more." Her gaze locked with his across the car's shadowy cabin. "And that kind of scares me, babe."

She reached for his hand. "You can talk to me about anything. You know that, right?"

Miles nodded. "I know this cool little diner—great coffee, best pie in town." He shrugged. "I mean, if that's all right with you?"

Vanessa studied his face for a moment and smiled. “Sure.”

“Okay, then.” Signaling left, he made a U-turn at the next intersection and started back the way they came. “Let’s go.”

11

Despite the late hour, Jimmy's Diner had a good number of patrons propped on the stools along its subway-tiled counter and tucked into its bright orange booths. Miles and Vanessa seated themselves in a secluded section in the back, where Miles ordered two cups of coffee and a slice of cherry pie for them to split, before folding his hands on top of the table and meeting Vanessa's eager gaze. "You gotta promise to keep an open mind and not freak out on me."

Smirking, she rolled her eyes and raised her right hand like she was getting ready to recite the Pledge of Allegiance. "I promise."

"What did you think of my friends tonight?" he asked.

Her smile faded. "Honestly, they looked like a gangsters and drug dealers."

"That's because they are, V. I mean, they're not the mafia or anything, but they live that lifestyle." He shrugged. "And I used to live it with them. In fact, they all used to work for me."

"Work for you?" Vanessa's voice was hushed, alarmed. She leaned forward, her wide eyes filled with a combination of concern and disbelief.

"Here we go." Their waitress seemed to appear out of nowhere. She set down their pie and two forks and poured them each a fresh cup of steaming coffee. "You just let me know if there's anything else you need."

Nodding her thanks, Vanessa waited for the waitress to walk out of earshot, before turning her attention back to Miles. "Work for you doing what?"

"I used to be a drug dealer, Vanessa. Those guys you met tonight, that was my crew. And basically, we was into any and everything."

"What do you mean?"

"We sold drugs, bought them, cooked them...you name it, we did it. And, it was a pretty big deal," he conceded with a tilt of his head. "We did a lot of business, made a lot of money."

Vanessa sat back, dazed. "I'm not sure what to say."

"Listen, I don't talk about it—I try not to even think about that time in my life—because I'm not proud of it. Honestly, I can't even remember how I got into it or why I did it, but I'm different now. I spent the last two years of my life just trying to shake that off, wash it away.

The earnestness in his eyes made her smile. "Wash it away, huh?"

"I'm a changed man, V."

"What about Marty? What about Chris, Wikki, Percy? Have they changed?"

"Believe me, I been telling those guys that there's more to life than slinging dope. That there are better ways—honest ways—to make a living. But they don't want to hear it."

"Well, baby, the Bible says that bad company corrupts good character." She arched a questioning brow. "You really think it's a wise idea still hanging out with these guys when they do what they do?"

"Those are my friends, V. Those dudes, they're like my family. I can count on them for anything," Miles said, his tone resolute. He sighed. "Look, I'll be the first to admit, I've still got growing to do. I mean, I'm not perfect—nowhere near it, but I'm trying, I'm working hard every day to be a better man."

Vanessa was quiet as she considered everything Miles had just revealed. "That was a mouthful," she finally said. "To be honest with you, babe, your story almost sounds like a testimony of someone who's been changed by God." Reaching across the table, she slipped her hand into his. "Thank you for even wanting to share this with me. Am I okay with it?" Vanessa shrugged. "I don't know about all that. Does it make me want to pull away? No," she said with a shake of her head. "If anything it makes me wanna get closer to you."

Caressing the back of her wrist with the tips of his fingers, Miles smiled. Just when he thought she couldn't prove any more amazing, Vanessa had found a way to exceed his expectations. "Would it be wrong to say that I'm falling in love with you?"

"No, baby." Smiling, she held his gaze. "Because I'm falling in love with you too."

Instinctively, they both leaned in and shared a sweet, tender kiss. When they parted, Miles sat back, feeling as though a two-ton boulder had just been lifted from his shoulders, and released a breath he hadn't realized he'd been holding. Vanessa laughed and heaved her own sigh of relief. She smirked. "Well, since you just had the floor, Scarface..."

"Oh, I'm Scarface now," Miles said with a chuckle.

"I guess it's my turn. Baby, do you know what equally yoked means?"

Miles tilted his head. "What you mean, like eggs or something?"

"No, silly." Vanessa laughed. "In the Bible, God refers to our spirits as equally yoked. So in order for you and me to be equally yoked," she said, pointing at him and then herself, "means that we have to feel the same about each other and about God. And we have to put Jesus in the center of this relationship." Vanessa searched his face, her eyes narrowed. "Do you think you can do that?"

He studied her intently. To be completely honest was to admit that he wasn't sure whether or not he was really up for the challenge. Vanessa was hardly the first woman in his life to talk to him about Christ and everything he stood to gain by developing a personal relationship with Him versus everything he stood to lose if he didn't. But church, the Bible, faith, prayer—none of those things had ever appealed to him. Partly because there were just too many unanswered questions out there—too much chaos, too much suffering, too many bad things happening to too many good people—for him to approach the notion of an omniscient higher power as anything more than a far-fetched ideology. And partly because, on the off chance that there really was a God and He really was all-knowing, all-seeing, the odds that His love and mercy extended to someone like Miles were slim to none.

Still Vanessa's acceptance of him regardless of his shortcomings and irrespective of his past was a gift that few others had offered and one that he had no plans to forgo.

"It sounds like a lot, babe. But I care about you enough to give it a try," he said.

And as he looked into her eyes, his amatory smile mirroring hers, he knew, without a doubt, that it was true.

Part Two

That Which Doesn't Kill

12

Miguel Leon was dutifully watering the neatly trimmed shrubs lining his front porch when he saw Miles coming up the walkway. He was urban dressed in a burgundy sports coat with notched lapels over a black twill button-down shirt and tailored trousers. Miguel took in his four-point pocket square and silk-knotted cuff links with an impressed hike of his brow.

"Well, don't you look dapper?"

Smiling, Miles shook his hand. "Thank you."

"So the big weekend is finally here."

"Yessir." Miles nodded. "This is it."

"Are these your events?"

"I got a few partners," he said with a shrug. "But for the most part, yeah, they're mine."

"Must be a good feeling to see all of your hard work paying off."

"It is—or, at least I hope it will be," he said, watching as Mr. Leon retracted the garden hose with a few turns of the reel at his feet. "I try not to count my chickens before they hatch."

Miguel dismissed Miles' attempt at propriety with a confidant nod of his head. "Well, if Vanessa's excitement is any indication, the whole thing's going to be a great success. She hasn't stopped talking about it since you invited her to go."

Miles' smile was automatic. They'd been together going on three months now, and he still couldn't see her, think about her, or even hear her name without his pulse quickening and his stomach fluttering.

Over the years he'd become somewhat notorious among his boys for changing girlfriends almost as often as he changed socks. Lauded as a modern-day Casanova, he'd fed into that reputation for a long while, wining and dining a seemingly endless carousel of women. And carelessly leaving a trail of hurt feelings and broken hearts in his wake.

Contrary to what anyone thought, though, Miles had never set out to be a womanizer, nor would he categorize himself as the proverbial playa. More than anything, he just wanted someone to share his time and, eventually, his life with. Someone who had more to offer than a cute face and a bangin' body. Someone with her own goals and opinions who would challenge and inspire him. Someone who wanted to grow with him and who could teach him things about the world and about himself.

But it seemed like the more he searched for what he wanted, the farther away he got from it. Until, eventually, he was caught in an unfulfilling cycle of dating and discarding—always chasing, always hunting, always striving to find in the next woman what the previous one was missing.

Then he met Vanessa. And his search abruptly came to an end. She embodied everything he wanted in a partner—brains, beauty, heart, and little bit of attitude mixed in for good measure. She wasn't afraid to call him on his stuff, but she also didn't hesitate to offer words of encouragement when she sensed he needed them. She was a woman about her business and yet she made a point of not taking herself too seriously. She was affectionate and attentive and she loved him not just for the man he was, but for the person he had the potential to be.

With each passing day, his feelings for her grew irrevocably stronger; and the longer he was with her, the more convinced he became that he never wanted to go back to life without her.

The sharp creak of the screen door opening and closing stirred Miles from his thoughts. He glanced up to see Vanessa, looking absolutely ravishing in a flirty lace cocktail dress and fire red pumps, smiling down at him from the top of the porch steps.

All of the last minute details and pressures of the impending weekend instantly shifted to the back of his mind as he held out his hand and she readily came to him.

"You two enjoy yourselves," Miguel said. "And be safe," he added in typical fatherly fashion.

Vanessa gave her dad a hug. "I'll call you later."

"Okay, sweetheart." He turned to Miles. "We'll say a prayer for you and your shows tonight."

"Thank you, Mr. Leon," Miles said. "I really appreciate it."

"You ready, babe?" Vanessa asked with an excited bounce.

He chuckled, buoyed by her ingenuous enthusiasm, and smoothly proffered his arm. "Let's hit it."

13

Vanessa gazed around the Fairmont's cavernous penthouse suite. Located at the very top of the hotel's famed tower, it boasted a fireplace, billiard room, library, and enormous picture windows that offered sweeping views of the city below. Sunny and stunningly well-appointed, the space, with its lush carpets, Frette linens and elegantly modern décor, was the picture of opulence.

From her comfy seat on one of the pillowy sofas, Vanessa watched the hub of frenetic activity taking place around her. Stationed in the formal dining room, Chris and Percy were busy confirming transportation arrangements for the artists, while Martin was in the master suite hammering out logistics with the security team. On the sprawling outdoor terrace, Wikki made last-minute accommodations for the evening's VIP guests and, in one of the sitting rooms off the parlor, T—a jovial, broad-shouldered man introduced to her as Miles' booking agent—punched numbers into a calculator as he combed through the preliminary ticket sales report.

It was a spectacular scene, one that rivaled any event she'd ever been part of, but even more impressive than the grand-scale production was the way Miles directed it with the flair and efficiency of a seasoned promoter.

"Looks good," he said, signing off on an invoice presented to him by one of several production assistants bustling about. He handed it back to her. "Do me a favor and see if the playbills have been delivered to the venue yet. Also, take these," he said, giving her a manila envelope. "They're copies of the backstage riders. Double-check all of the dressing rooms.

Make sure they haven't overlooked any of the artists' special requests. And be sure to call me on the suite's extension if there are any problems."

"You got it," she said, heading for the door.

"Tams!" he bellowed.

Vanessa looked up to see a statuesque woman carrying a clipboard and donning a headset quickly making her way across the long parlor. Vanessa stood as Miles met her halfway and greeted her with a kiss on the cheek.

"What's going on? How we looking?"

"Everything looks great," she said, handing him a sheaf of paperwork. "All the groups are checked into the hotel. Sound checks going on right now. Looks like you got yourself a sellout."

"That's what I'm talking about," he said.

She sidestepped Miles and offered Vanessa a warm handshake. "You must be Ms. Leon." She smiled. "It's a pleasure to finally meet you. Miles talks about you all the time."

"Oh yeah, sorry," he said, distractedly glancing up from the pages in his hand. "V, this is Tamara. She makes it all go, as you can see."

"Nice to meet you. And please, call me Vanessa."

"Listen, if you need anything at all in the next couple of days," Tamara said. "You just let me know, all right?"

Vanessa nodded. "Thanks, I will."

"Do you have your will call list ready?" Tamara asked, turning her attention back to Miles. He'd traded the papers she'd given him for his cell phone and was scribbling notes as he listened intently to the person on the other end.

"Hang on one second," he said, putting the caller on hold. Handing Tamara an edited roster, he pointed to the bottom of the page. "You see these last names, right here? Make sure they get in for me, would you?"

Tamara nodded. "I sure will. Anything else before I whisk her way?" she asked, gesturing toward Vanessa.

Vanessa glanced between the two of them, confused. "Whisk me away to where?"

"I might've planned a little something for you," Miles said with a devilish grin.

She smiled. "A little something like what?"

"Well, if I told you, it wouldn't be a surprise, now, would it?" he asked, brushing aside her hair and kissing her forehead.

"You didn't have to do this," she said. "Whatever it is."

He shrugged. "I hated the idea of you cooped up here all day."

She glanced around the palatial suite. "I'd hardly call this cooped up," she said with a laugh. "But thank you."

"All right. So we will see you a little later." Tamara said, motioning for Vanessa to follow her. "And you should probably get back to work." She pointed at the cell phone still in his hand.

"You take good care of my baby."

"Not to worry," Tamara said, offering them both a reassuring smile. "She's in good hands."

Vanessa grabbed her camera and her room key from her purse and followed Tamara out of the suite and down the long corridor to the elevators. "So, are you going to tell me where we're going?" she asked.

"Not a chance." Tamara shook her head and laughed. "But one thing I *can* tell you, is that you're in for a real treat," she said just as the doors opened with a ding. Tamara stepped aside so that Vanessa could board first, then pressed the button for the hotel's Terrace Level.

"Have you worked with Miles long?"

Tamara nodded. "Going on six years, now. He's a great boss—a great guy in general. And he's absolutely crazy about you."

Face flushed, Vanessa smiled. "The feeling's definitely mutual."

In truth, Miles was proving to be the single best surprise of her life. Never in a million years did she think she would have fallen head over heels for someone like him—a reformed bad boy who lived in a mansion, tooled around in a car that cost more than her house, and hung out with known drug dealers. Her last boyfriend had been a minister in training and her boyfriend before that a preacher's kid. But Miles, he hadn't stepped foot inside a church since he was a teenager. He wasn't a man of faith, couldn't recite a hymn, didn't know a single passage from the Bible. He didn't fit the mold of the guy she was supposed to love, he completely reinvented it. "The whole thing was just so unexpected," Vanessa mused out loud.

Tamara smiled. "I find the best things in life always are."

Arriving on their floor, Tamara disembarked and led Vanessa through a maze of doorways and down a wide hallway at the end of which was the entrance to the hotel's spa.

The woman manning the reception desk smiled brightly as they entered. "Hello, ladies. I'm Kate. How can I help you today?"

"Yes. I'm Tamara Campbell—Mr. Montego's assistant. We spoke earlier."

Her eyes widening with recognition, Kate stood. "Of course," she said, hastily rounding the large desk between them. "Your room is ready and the rest of your party has already arrived."

"Rest of my party?" Vanessa asked, raising a quizzical brow in Tamara's direction.

Tamara offered Vanessa a cagy grin as she turned to leave. "Enjoy."

"I'll show you to the changing area," Kate said, ushering her through an ornate archway flanked with pillars. Coming to a stop in front of a large glass door, she handed Vanessa a key. "There's a complementary robe in your locker," she said. "Once you're ready, you can head straight to the last room on the right."

Following Kate's directions, Vanessa traded her dress and heels for a plush terry cloth robe and fuzzy slippers, then made her way to the end of the hallway. A gold-plated sign on the door read, *Treatment Room 1.* Beneath it, a sliding tab indicated that the room was in use.

Vanessa leaned in and listened closely. She could hear voices coming from the other side. Thinking that Kate assigned her the wrong room, she went back to the front desk to double- check, but no one was there. Reluctantly, she returned to the closed door and knocked.

"Come in," trilled a familiar voice.

Vanessa turned the knob and peeked her head inside. "What in the world?" she squealed, a shocked smile spreading across her face.

Inside, Heather and Kristi were sporting matching robes and sipping Mimosas. "Surprise!" they shouted in unison.

"What are you guys doing here?" Vanessa asked, rushing to give them both a hug.

Kristi pointed to the three massage tables set up in the middle of the room. "What does it look like?" she asked, her eyes wide with excitement. "We're here for a spa day!"

14

Their spa day turned out to be a no-holds-barred afternoon of indulgent pampering. Massages were followed by facials and then mani-pedis, after which they were escorted to The Grill on the Alley. There they enjoyed a leisurely lunch before being whisked away to a Tower Suite reserved for them by Miles, where their very own makeup artist and hairstylist helped get them glammed up for the night's event.

"Hands down, this has been the best day..." Heather said, reclining against the leather seats of the limo chauffeuring them to the venue, "...like, of my entire life."

"Seriously," Kristi said. "I thought stuff like this only happened in the movies."

"I feel like *Pretty Woman.*" Heather examined her reflection for the tenth time in as many minutes. "Minus the whole hooker thing," she amended, snapping shut her compact.

Vanessa laughed. "I'm just thankful you guys are here," she said. "I can't think of anyone else I would've rather experienced this with."

"Don't thank us." Heather grinned. "Thank that amazing boyfriend of yours."

Kristi nodded. "Amazing isn't the word."

"Does he have a brother?" Heather asked with a hopeful lilt.

"Nope. Only child."

Heather rolled her eyes in mock disgust. "The good ones always are."

"He's a keeper," Kristi said. "Hang on to him."

Vanessa smiled. "I plan to."

The limo turned onto South First Street and came to a stop in front of the California Theatre. MILES MONTEGO PRESENTS OLD-SCHOOL FUNK FEST flashed in bright lights on the marquee above the entrance. And behind red velvet ropes extending from either side of the glass ticket booth, two long lines of people stretched around the building and down the block.

Their driver opened the door and when Vanessa stepped onto the curb, Miles was there waiting for her. "Wow," he said, his sweeping gaze admiring her from head to toe. For the show, she'd slipped into an off-the-shoulder bandage dress and a pair of sequined sling backs. The makeup artist Miles hired had given her smoky eyes and sultry red lips. And, courtesy of the hairstylist, her usually curly locks fell in sleek strands against her back.

"I'm speechless," Miles said, giving her a twirl.

She took in his sharp black vested suit. "You clean up pretty nice yourself."

"Ladies." Miles smiled at Heather and Kristi. "You both look beautiful."

"Thank you for everything," Heather said, leaning in so she could be heard above the noisy crowd. "Today was a lot of fun."

"Well, it ain't over yet. Come on." Placing an affectionate hand on the small of Vanessa's back, he nodded toward the bright lights of the theatre. "We got the best seats in the house."

Miles and Vanessa returned to the Fairmont well after midnight. Now empty, except for them, the penthouse suite seemed even bigger to Vanessa as she kicked her heels off and headed to the master bedroom for a nice, long shower.

Flipping on the light, Vanessa paused to admire her makeover in the bathroom's gilded mirror. She smiled nostalgically, almost sad to have to wash away the makings of such a storybook day. Wiggling out of her dress, she threw her hair back into a ponytail and stepped into the walk-in shower. Steam filled the small stall as the power jets pelted her skin and her mind drifted back to her evening with Miles.

He'd kept a protective arm around her for most of the night, showing her off to old friends and business partners alike as they mingled among the attendees in the theatre's chandeliered lobby before the show started. Every so often Miles would press his lips to her ear and whisper how beautiful she was, sending a smile to her face and shiver down her spine.

Upon the blinking of the house lights, they headed, hand in hand, to the dress circle, where they joined Heather, Kristi, T, and the rest of the crew already settled into one of the rows of cushioned chairs, chatting and flipping through their playbills.

What followed was a veritable lineup of arguably the best old-school music groups to ever grace the stage. The Gap Band, Ohio Players, Brothers Johnson, Commodores, George Clinton, Kool and the Gang—all the pioneers of funk gathered for one night in San Jose and she had a front row seat.

Happily humming a tune from one of the performances, Vanessa turned off the shower and padded into the bedroom, where she dried off. Rooting through her suitcase in search of a pair of pajamas, she was surprised to come across one of Miles' track suits. Smiling to herself, she put it on and threw open the door to the living room. "Yo, yo, yo. What's good?" she asked, tiling up her chin and folding her arms across her chest like an old school rapper.

Miles looked up from the receipts scattered across the coffee table and laughed as she approached the couch with an exaggerated lean in her step. "I'm the one and only, Miles Montego," she said, voice pitched low. "Ain't no question."

"And who are you supposed to be?" he asked, eyeing her outfit. To him, she looked just as sexy in his old sweats as she did all done up.

"You!" Smiling, she plopped down beside.

He chuckled. "That is not how I act or talk or any of that."

Vanessa shrugged. "It's my manly ways," she said with a laugh. "Listen, babe, I just want to tell you that today was incredible. And I'm not just talking about what you did for me. I'm talking about you." Cupping the side of his face in her hand, she caressed his cheek. "You were amazing. Like, honestly, I was so impressed with how the whole show came together."

"Really?" he asked, covering her hand with his.

Nodding, she smiled as he left a trail of kisses up her arm. His mouth traveled from her shoulder to her neck and chin, then to her lips. Unlike all their kisses before, this one was strong, passionate. She felt her breath catch as he pulled her in one swift movement onto his lap and his fingers traveled up her back and tangled in her hair.

"We should probably get some rest," she whispered, pulling away, before the urge to give in to temptation overcame her. Standing, she started for the master suite. Miles followed. "Where do you think you're going?" Vanessa asked, raising a questioning brow.

He pointed past her to the bedroom. "To sleep?"

Vanessa laughed. "Uh, no. See that's my room," she said, tossing her thumb over her shoulder. "Lucky for you, Mr. Montego, this penthouse has two other bedrooms for you to pick from. Or you can stick with the couch." Smiling, she shrugged. "Either way, I get the king-size bed."

He shook his head in protest. "Yeah, but I thought—"

"Love ya. Don't forget to say your prayers," she added, blowing him a kiss before she disappeared behind her bedroom door.

Miles stood frozen for a moment, dumbfounded by what had just happened. Then, with a chuckle and shake of his head, he made his way down the hall to take a long, cold shower.

15

Saturday started with a delicious continental breakfast taken on the penthouse suite's private terrace. Miles and Vanessa sipped fresh-squeezed orange juice and fed each other warm croissants as they planned out their day once they arrived in San Francisco. More than anything, Vanessa wanted to walk the Golden Gate Bridge and ride one of the city's world famous cable cars. First on Miles' agenda was a shopping excursion at Union Square.

Though she'd lived in San Jose her entire life, Vanessa had never made the hour-long trip north. Along with New York and Paris, the Golden City had long topped her list of places to someday visit, a fact that made the pleasantly scenic ride even more enjoyable. With his shades on and his window down, Miles sang along to the radio while Vanessa snapped candid photos from the passenger's seat, capturing moments that were already turning into cherished memories.

Once they arrived, the two wasted no time checking into their hotel and hitting the streets. The city was a vibrant vision of rolling hills, colorful buildings, and historical landmarks all set against a backdrop of blue skies and glistening water. The people, eccentric and diverse, were friendly and free spirited.

They found their way to popular Alamo Square in the Haight-Ashbury district, where they took turns posing in front of the famous Painted Ladies on Steiner Street, then grabbed a quick bite to eat at one of the quaint outdoor cafes before riding a cable car to Union Square.

Like a kid in a candy store, Miles treated himself and Vanessa to a whirlwind shopping spree, lavishing them both to his heart's content and arranging for all the shops to deliver their spoils to the hotel downtown.

From Union Square, the two took the short stroll to Mission and Fifth Streets and caught a Golden Gate Transit bus to the south end of the bridge. The viewing points offered breathtaking landscapes of the sailboat-speckled Bay abutting the city's imposing skyline. At Vanessa's insistence, they took a personally guided tour where they learned the history and science behind the fascinating structure and snapped pictures of everything from the signs to the steel rivets.

With a little time left to spare before they had to get ready for Miles' show, they hailed a cab to Market Street where they bought ice cream cones and held hands as they watched the sky turn from blue to pink to red and the sun set behind the Ferry Building.

"Yo, we should really get going," Miles said, glancing at his watch. He smirked. "Can't be late to my own party."

"I know. All good things must come to an end." Vanessa sighed. "I'm really gonna miss this place. But, on the bright side," she said, smiling up at him. "I finally get to cross San Fran off my bucket list."

"You got a bucket list?" Miles arched a curious brow. "How come you ain't ever mentioned it before?"

Vanessa shrugged. "It's not a big deal. Mostly just a bunch of places I hope to visit someday. You know, the Eiffel Tower, Niagara Falls. Statue of Liberty's probably my number one."

"Uh oh, okay. The Big Apple."

"I've wanted to go there from the time I was a kid—ever since I saw *Home Alone 2*." She simpered. "Corny, right?"

"Nah, it ain't corny. It's sweet." Miles wrapped an arm around her shoulders. "And I'm glad you told me. Now that I know about this list, I think Imma have to take you to New York next—show you what it's all about."

Vanessa laughed. "Just name the time and the place and I'll be there, bags packed."

"It's a date, then."

She glanced up at him, her expression wistful. "You promise?"

Miles met her gaze with a gentle smile and a nod. "Ain't no question."

~

"I don't know how you did it, babe. But I actually think this show might've been better than the last one, if that's even possible," Vanessa said, fastening her seatbelt.

"I think you might be right." Miles started his car and backed it out of his reserved space in VIP parking. "I mean, the San Jose crowd was great, but tonight's audience—"

"Was hype!" Vanessa said, taking the words right out if his mouth. "They gave it a standing ovation! And can you believe the closing act gave two encores? Two!" she squealed excitedly.

Laughing, Miles nodded. "Tams said it was another sellout."

"And another great day for the books," she said, sitting back with a contented sigh. "Hey, what time do we have to head out tomorrow? I was thinking maybe we could go check out Fisherman's Wharf since we didn't have time today."

"What's going on here?" Miles, asked distracted by something in the distance.

Vanessa followed his line of sight as the car slowed, straining to see across the empty venue parking lot, lit only by a few towering lamp posts. As Miles crept closer she could make out Martin and Chris arguing with two men.

"Get out the car, homie!" Martin shouted. He pounded relentlessly on the dented hood. "Get out the car!"

"Don't do it," Miles murmured, his eyes trained on the scene ahead.

"Oh my God, Miles. What's happening?" Vanessa asked.

"Open it, Jessie!" Martin barked, kicking the door. When the driver refused to come out, Martin shattered the glass with one blow of his elbow and dragged the guy through the bent frame of the window. "I told you to get out of the car, punk!"

Vanessa watched horrified as Martin threw Jessie to the ground and he and Chris began punching and kicking him mercilessly.

By the time Jessie's passenger had rounded the car with his gun drawn, Miles had already popped open his glove compartment and grabbed a weapon of his own.

"Miles don't do it," Vanessa pleaded. "Don't do it, Miles."

"Lock the door and get down," he ordered, quickly exiting his vehicle and making his way toward the standoff.

Shaking, she obeyed and watched, her heart racing, as Miles crept up on Jessie's homeboy and pistol whipped him across the back of the head. Dazed by the impact, the guy dropped his gun. Miles picked it up and aimed one weapon at Jessie and the other at Jessie's friend.

"Yeah, wassup now, dogg?" Martin asked as he and Chris joined Miles. "You ain't so tough now, are you?"

"Back up!" Miles shouted. "Back up!"

Jessie and his homeboy raised their hands and eased away.

Miles kept a barrel trained on each of them. "Is there a problem, Jessie? Is there?"

"Nah, we straight." Jessie's smirk was sinister. "Ain't no problem here?"

"Man, Miles, just shoot this punk," Chris said. "Finish him!"

Martin nodded. "Shoot him, Miles!"

Crying, Vanessa swiped at the tears streaming down her checks and sunk farther into the front passenger seat of Miles' Bentley.

Miles shook his head. "Ain't nobody gonna get shot tonight. But what y'all are gonna do," he said, addressing Jessie and his friend, "is get into that car and get outta here. Ain't that right?" Miles asked, his voice escalating. Stepping closer, he held the guns just inches from their faces. "Get in your car and get outta here! Now!" he shouted.

Scrambling, Jessie and his cohort got into the car and slammed the doors behind them. "This ain't over," Jessie warned through the hole where his window used to be. "Watch your back."

"See you around, homie," Chris called as Jessie revved his engine and sped off into the night.

"Yo, dogg, thanks for looking out," Martin said, turning to Miles.

"Come on, man. You know I always got your back." Miles handed Martin Jessie's gun. "Look, take care of this."

"I got you," Martin said, already headed for his Hummer.

Miles pointed at Chris. "Go with him."

The two men jumped into Martin's SUV as Miles rushed back to his car. Throwing it into gear, he peeled out of the parking lot behind Martin and Chris and headed straight for their hotel.

16

Sobbing, Vanessa's stormed into their hotel suite and sat on the edge of the bed. Pulling her knees to her chest, she hid her face behind her hands with a shudder.

"Baby, are you all right?" Miles asked, kneeling on the floor beside her. "Baby, talk to me," he pleaded, tugging at her elbow.

Still crying, Vanessa snatched her arm away.

"Are you okay?" he asked again. "Babe!"

"No, I'm not okay, Miles!" She looked up, her eyes watery, her cheeks streaked with tears and mascara. Combing her fingers through her tousled hair, she glared at him. "Who were those guys? Were they trying to kill you?"

"Baby, just relax," Miles said soothingly. "I was just trying to diffuse the situation."

"It had nothing to do with you!" she shrieked. "It was between Martin and whoever that guy was."

"So what was I supposed to do?" Miles asked. "Leave him out there alone? Let some dude just blow his head off? Is that what you're telling me?" He shook his head. "I don't think so, babe."

The mattress squeaked beneath Vanessa's shifting weight. "So, you're willing to give up everything, including your own life, for something that had nothing to do with you?"

"Yes!" he exclaimed loudly. "And they would do the same for me." Miles sighed. "Baby, look," he said after a few moments, his voice decidedly calmer. "A few years ago, this whole thing would have turned out a lot different."

Vanessa shook her head and looked away.

"I was just trying to get us out of there safe," he insisted. "That's it."

"Really? Then would you like to tell me why there was a gun in your car?" Her question echoed throughout the small space of the room.

"I already told you, babe. Whenever I do shows like this, there's always large amounts of cash around. You know that! You see it!" Frustrated, he popped open the briefcase resting at the foot of the bed. Inside was tens of thousands of dollars, stacked and wrapped in neat bundles. "Look!"

Vanessa refused.

"What do want me to do?" he asked, slamming the case shut. "Listen." Inching closer, he wrapped his arms around her. "I know this whole situation—everything that's happening—is all new to you. But you gotta understand, V. When it comes to protecting you, my family, my friends… I'll do anything, babe." He felt her relax into his embrace.

"I thought I was gonna lose you," she sniffled.

"C'mon, baby," he said, stroking her back.

"No. Really, Miles," her voice cracked. "I don't wanna feel that way again. Ever." Wriggling loose from his grip, she sat back and held his gaze with her own. "Promise me I'll never lose you."

"I promise," he said, wiping away her tears as they fell from her chin. "I ain't going nowhere."

Vanessa edged closer. "Give me your hands." Miles obeyed as she bowed her head. "Heavenly Father," she began. "Thank You for your watch, care, and protection over us. We come before You, grateful for a wonderful day spent together. And we give You praise for another successful event. Be with Miles. Continue to teach him, guide him, and show him that You are with him always. In Your name we pray. Amen."

Miles lifted his head, surprised by the mist in his eyes and smiled. "Amen."

17

"Woooo!" Vanessa hooted as her family finished singing the last few bars of "Happy Birthday" to Miles. Everyone clapped and Vanessa raised her camera. "Smile, baby," she said while lining up the perfect shot, before snapping a photo of him grinning in front of his cake.

Miles looked around the table at Vanessa, her parents, and two sisters. "Thank you guys, really." He looked around their cute, little kitchen decorated with balloons, a homemade banner and streamers. "You didn't have to do this," he said, touched. "I appreciate it."

"Oh, stop," Julissa said with a smile.

Alyssa nodded. "We wanted to."

"Now, Miles, the family bought you a little something," Miguel said, producing an exquisitely wrapped box from beneath he table. He set it in front of Miles. "We hope that you'll not only use it, but enjoy it as well."

"Wow." He looked at the gift and then at their expectant faces. "Now this is too much, right here," he said, smiling. "You did not have to do all this."

"Go on. Open it!" Alyssa said.

"Yeah." Julissa clapped her hands excitedly. "Hurry up!"

"Okay, okay." Laughing, Miles untied the ribbon and removed the top. Resting inside was a leather-bound Bible. His name was embossed in gold lettering across the cover. "Get outta here!" he said, taking it out of the box. "You guys got me my own Bible!"

"Let me get a picture." Vanessa aimed her camera as Miles posed. "Love it!"

Lydia Leon, who was seated next to her husband, regarded Miles frostily. "Try not to use it as a coaster," she sniffed.

The jovial conversation taking place around the table came to an awkward halt.

"No, of course not." Miles shook his head. "Never that. This is going right upstairs on my nightstand," he assured her.

She didn't look comforted. "Well, hopefully, you can find some time between concert promoting and weekend getaways with my daughter to actually read it."

It had been several weeks since Miles and Vanessa's trip and a day hadn't yet gone by that they didn't spend hours talking on the phone, or when Vanessa's work and school schedules permitted, hanging out at each other's houses. But despite Miles' increasingly regular presence, Lydia Leon had yet to warm up to him. Generally, she made her disapproval known by ignoring him altogether, no matter how polite or solicitous he was. And on the rare occasions when she was forced to endure his company, she sat stonily in the shadows and spoke as little as possible.

"Come on Lydia," Miguel patted his wife's knee, "it's a celebration."

"Well excuse me if I'm more concerned about making sure that he's the right one than I am about unwrapping gifts and blowing out candles."

"Mom," Vanessa pleaded.

"No...it's okay," Miles said. He turned to Lydia. "Go ahead, Mrs. Leon."

"You need to understand something, Miles. We have done everything we can do," she said, pointing at herself and Miguel. "To raise our daughters in the way of the Lord."

He looked at Vanessa. "I can see that."

"The Bible says we should pray for our children's spouses early in their lives," Lydia continued. "And for their future partners, that they will be equally yoked." She narrowed her eyes. "Do you know what that means?"

"Yeah. Well, sorta." Miles shrugged. "V and I, we've talked about it—you know, the importance of feeling the same way about God and each other."

Lydia nodded.

"We've been praying for a godly man for Vanessa for a long time," she said, studying him. Her gaze was unflinching. "Are you that godly man?"

Miles considered her question. He loved Vanessa more than he could ever say. And her faith was important to him, because it was such a big part of her life. Whereas religion had never before been a factor, he could now admit to being curious about Jesus and intrigued by the prospect of having a personal relationship with Him.

Vanessa spoke of God some days as though He was her most trusted confidant—a best friend who never failed her and never left her side. As someone who had always been the shot caller, who was always expected to have the answers, the idea of surrendering to something and someone greater than him was strangely comforting to Miles. But a passing compulsion hardly qualified him as a godly man.

When it came to Vanessa, he knew he didn't measure up to her mother's expectations. But the bigger question at hand—did he measure up to God's?

He shook his head and lowered his gaze with a sigh. "I don't know."

18

"That smells good," Vanessa said. Abandoning her post at the cutting board, where she was slicing tomatoes for their salads, she rounded the island toward the stove to take a peek over Miles' shoulder.

"Hey. Get outta here." He angled himself to block her view as he flipped the salmon steak sizzling in the skillet in front of him. "I can't have you stealing my secret recipes."

"Hold up," she said, her brow raised, her hip jutted. "I'll admit, you got mad skills in the kitchen, but nobody throws down better than I do."

"Oh, really?" He smirked as he turned to face her. "That sounds like a challenge to me."

"Anytime you're ready to get schooled, Mr. Montego. You know where to find me."

"Yeah, okay. Watch it with that," he said, stepping back. His eyes followed the blade of the knife still in her hand. "This ain't an episode of 'Snapped.'"

Laughing, they both returned to cooking. The quiet between them was comfortable, the mood familiar as they prepared dinner together.

"Hey, babe. After church tomorrow, I was thinking maybe we could catch a movie?"

Miles winced. "About tomorrow, baby," he said, his tone apologetic, "I don't think I'm going to be able to make it."

He'd managed to weasel out of going to church the previous Sunday and the Sunday before that, but Vanessa's chilly silence told him that he was out of strikes. "What's the matter, babe? You okay?"

"No Miles, I'm not," she said, slamming down the knife. "Look, just tell me what the problem is."

Miles turned to face her again. "There is no problem, babe. I just have some things to take care of, that's all."

"We all have a lot of stuff we have to do. You're always gonna have a lot of things you have to do!" Vanessa took a calming breath. "Look, I'm gonna put aside the fact that my entire family is expecting you. And hey," she shrugged, "I'd actually like you to come to church with me. What I'm really concerned with is what the real issue is. Why don't you just tell me?"

Shaking his head, he returned his attention to the stove. "There's nothing to tell."

"Really. There's nothing to tell?" she asked, sounding utterly unconvinced. "I'm not buying that."

Miles whipped back around. "Look, what do you want from me?"

"I want you to tell me the truth."

"The truth about what, V?"

"Why you refuse to go to church?"

"Cuz God don't want somebody like me in His church!" Miles shouted. "Okay?"

Vanessa's expression softened. Tilting her head, she smiled.

"I'm glad you think it's funny," he said.

Wordlessly, Vanessa made her way to him and wrapped her arms around his waist. "Look, babe. I'm not trying to belittle your feelings," she said, resting her weight against his chest. "But you are just so off. Like, so off." She chuckled. "To be honest, I'm kind of relieved. I thought you were actually keep something from me, something ugly."

"Yeah, well, don't be getting all happy just yet. I haven't told you why I feel this way."

"It doesn't matter." Leaning back, she met his worried gaze with a shake of her head. "God doesn't care about what you've done in the past or what you're in the middle of right now. He just wants you to come as you are."

"You sure about that?"

"I'm positive. Look, the Bible says, 'what good is it for a man to gain the whole world and lose his soul?' Baby, I don't want you to lose your soul." She cradled the side of his face in her hand. "Once you really get to know God and His word you'll see that Book is better than life."

"Better than life, huh?"

She nodded. "Better than the cars, better than the money, and for a man like you, better than..." Giggling, she let her sentence trail off and made her way back to the cutting board.

"Better than what?"

"Better than sex." She glanced up at him. "Yes! I said it."

He chuckled. "Well, then, you're right. This must be a *great* book, cuz ain't too many things better than—"

"Hey! Watch what you say." Smirking, Vanessa wagged the knife at him. "We're talking about God—better than anything. Don't get crazy."

Laughing, they went back to cooking, each of them quietly in suspense of what the next day would hold.

19

Evergreen Valley Church sat at the center of a beautifully landscaped campus tucked into the southeastern foothills of San Jose. A massive structure surrounded by a sea of cars, Miles thought he'd misunderstood Vanessa when she'd told him to turn into the packed parking lot. But for the gold cross perched atop the domed roof's towering steeple, the place looked more like a venue for one of his concerts than it did a place of worship.

Maneuvering his Bentley into an empty space, Miles grabbed his new Bible from the backseat and made his way with Vanessa toward the entrance.

"You ready, babe?" she asked, bumping him playfully as they walked.

"As ready as I'm gonna get." He looked around at the cliques of people migrating from all directions toward the open doors. "This is crazy, though. It looks like a sold-out show."

She smiled. "It is, Miles. It's the greatest show on earth. And it's free."

Just as they reached the tree-lined sidewalk, a white Lamborghini cruised by them and pulled into one of the reserved parking spots ahead. Slowing his pace, Miles watched a man decked out in a white Yankees baseball cap, a crisp white button down shirt, and dark wash jeans step out and onto the curb. Sporting a sizeable diamond stud in his left earlobe and a conspicuous cross pendant on a long, gold chain around his neck, he looked like a cat Miles might have a drink with at the club, not a man of faith who reported to church on Sunday mornings.

His presence was strangely magnetic, his swagger undeniable as he closed his car's butterfly door and headed up the covered walkway. He noticed Miles watching him from across the lot and held his gaze for a moment before nodding hello and disappearing into the building.

"Come on, babe. Let's go," Vanessa said, holding out her hand.

Miles took it, and together they made their way inside the church and across the lobby to the sanctuary. Standing at the doors, a tall gentleman dressed in a suit welcomed them with a bulletin and a smile. "Good morning, Vanessa. How are you doing today?"

"I'm good, Jerry. This is my boyfriend, Miles," she said, introducing Miles with a proud glint in her eye. "Baby, this is Jerry."

"Pleasure to meet you, Miles." He shook his hand, then motioned for Vanessa to follow him. "I'll seat you with your parents."

Miles waited for Jerry to walk out of earshot, before leaning close to Vanessa. "Am I supposed to tip this guy?"

Vanessa laughed. "No, baby. He doesn't get paid. He's an usher," she explained. "This is his way of serving the Lord."

Miles took in his surroundings as they walked. He felt his muscles relax and his nerves ease. Inside, the sanctuary looked nothing like the spooky brick cathedral he'd attended as a child. There were no stuffy archways, column pillars, and creepy murals of patron saints painted on cold stone walls. No hard wooden pews or cold marble floors or votive candles burning in front of solemn statues. He saw no one crossing themselves or genuflecting before the altar. No one burning incense or dabbing holy water or talking to their neighbors in reverent whispers.

Instead, people lined the wide aisles and the packed rows chatting and laughing among themselves. Spacious and bright, the place looked like a stadium with cushioned theatre seats and airy ceilings. Spotlights and speakers hung from rafters above and two Jumbotrons, one on either side of the crescent stage, flashed the weekly announcements. Behind the pulpit a band of musicians tuned their instruments and singers situated themselves in groups around a line of microphones. Squinting, Miles took a closer look at the gathering praise team. Vanessa's younger sister, Alyssa, was among them. She spotted Miles and waved. Smiling, he waved back.

"Here we are," Jerry said, showing them to a row of seats just a few feet from the stage. Miguel and Lydia Leon were seated with Julissa. The Leons stood when they saw Miles and Vanessa approaching.

"Hi, Mom," Vanessa said, greeting Lydia with a kiss on the cheek.

"Good to see you, Miles." Miguel reached past his wife and daughter to shake Miles' hand. "You look like a million bucks in that suit."

"Thank you. Good to see you too, Mr. Leon." He smiled at Vanessa's mom. "How you doing, Mrs. Leon?"

Lydia looked him up and down with discontented sigh. "Good morning, Miles."

As they took their seats, Miles noticed the Holstons waving from the row ahead of them. "Hey, Karen." Smiling, he pointed. "I see you Nicky."

The lights overhead dimmed and the stage brightened as the band started playing and a familiar face ascended the stage steps. It was the man who'd pulled up outside in the white Lamborghini. Microphone in hand, he started to sing.

Miles turned to Vanessa. "Who's that?"

"That's Pastor Galley," she said. "He's our worship leader."

"He's a *pastor?*" Miles asked, his surprise plain. He watched Pastor Galley pace from one end of the platform to the other, his mellow voice echoing throughout the yawning space. As the music swelled, the worship team behind him joined in, their voices harmonizing, while the lyrics to "Worthy of All Praise" scrolled across both Jumbotrons. All around him people sang along, clapping and swaying to the beat.

Pastor Galley led the congregation in several more upbeat worship songs, after which another parishioner made his way to the pulpit. He took a moment to welcome all of the visitors, before reading a short passage from the Bible and saying an impassioned prayer.

Once he'd returned to his seat, a soloist from the worship team replaced Pastor Galley at the lead mic. Accompanied by the band, her melodic voice filled the air as she belted a ballad of praise to the Lord.

While she sang, the ushers stood in the aisles and sent blue velvet bags down the rows. As the bags passed from one seat to the next, people dropped envelopes inside. When it was his turn to give, Miles pulled a thick fold of cash from his pocket and counted some off the top.

"Babe," Vanessa whispered. "Everyone doesn't need to see that." She nodded at the wad of money in his hand.

"Oh, my bad," he said. Lowering it, he peeled off a few more bills.

Vanessa's eyes widened. "How much are you giving?"

"Like this much," he said, holding up a few hundred dollars. "What, not enough?"

"Babe, that's plenty." Vanessa pat his knee with a laugh. "I'll explain how this whole offering thing works later."

Soon afterward, the sermon followed. With Vanessa's help, Miles used his Bible to follow along. Though at times the New Testament parable they studied read more like a riddle than a story, he listened carefully and gleaned a lot from Pastor Tim's talk about using his God-given talents to serve the Lord. The notion of God requiring much from those who'd been given much intrigued him. And he was surprised to find himself, even after they'd been dismissed, thinking of ways he might apply the points from the message to his everyday life.

On their stroll back to his car, they ran into Pastor Galley, just as he was ending a conversation with a woman Miles recognized from the praise team.

"Hey, Pastor Galley," Vanessa said as they approached. "How are you?"

"What's up, ma? How you doing?" He gave her a hug.

"Blessed." She smiled. "Pastor Galley, I wanted to introduce you to my boyfriend, Miles." Vanessa stepped aside as the shook hands.

"Miles, you got some church in today, huh?"

"Yeah." He nodded. "It wasn't what I was expecting, but it was good."

Pastor Galley smiled. "That's right."

"Hey, so…" Miles paused, not sure how to tactfully phrase the question that had been burning in the back of his mind since he'd seen him singing on stage. "You're really a pastor? I mean, like a *real* pastor?"

Pastor Galley laughed. "You mean as opposed to an imaginary, cartoon pastor?"

"Nah, man. That's not what I meant." He shrugged. "You just don't look like a pastor, that's all."

"I don't, huh?" Pastor Galley smirked. "What's a real pastor supposed to look like?"

Miles thought about his question for a moment. "I don't know," he said. "But, I mean, look at you, man—your clothes and jewelry."

Pastor Galley smiled. "You kinda tight to def yourself there too, Miles."

"Yeah, but I don't drive no Lambo, Pastor."

"Lambo, huh?" He narrowed his eyes. "I recall pulling into the parking lot and passing a black Bentley that I've never seen here before. I'm assuming that's yours."

Miles chuckled. "Yeah, but I ain't no pastor."

"True that. But the last time I read the Bible, it said nothing about style being a sin. Kind of goes back to that old say, 'don't judge a book by its cover,' ya heard?"

"Yeah, I dig." Miles tilted his head. "So what made you want to be pastor, anyway?"

"Well, God had a calling on my life, Miles. And as much as I tried to avoid that call, I couldn't run from it any longer." Pastor Galley shrugged. "So, here I am. He's got a calling on your life too," he said, pointing at Miles. "On everybody's life. But you gotta answer the phone when He calls, ya dig?"

"A calling," Miles echoed.

"That's right, a calling. I'll tell you what. We'll talk more about it in the future." Pastor Galley smiled. "I'd love to see you around here a little bit more."

Miles nodded. "All right."

"All right," he said. "Vanessa, you have a blessed Sunday."

"You do the same." Smiling, she gave him another hug. "Such good worship today, by the way."

"Praise God!" Pastor Galley said. Turning back to Miles, he shook his hand. "It was a real pleasure."

"No. Pastor..." he said, meeting his meaningful gaze with a grateful smile. "...the pleasure was all mine."

~

Not wanting to waste the beautiful day ahead of them, Miles took Vanessa to one of his favorite lunch spots downtown. After a great meal and leisurely stroll, they found themselves sitting in the park at Caesar Chavez Plaza. Their fingers intertwined, Vanessa casually draped one of her legs over Miles' knee as they soaked in the sun and enjoyed the breeze.

"Hey, babe." Vanessa was first to break the contended silence that had settled over them. "You know when Pastor Tim gave the altar call at the end of service today?"

"Yeah." Miles nodded and waited for her to continue.

"Would you ever consider, you know, taking that walk of faith?"

"I don't know," Miles sighed. "I'm not gonna lie, babe. I'm still trying to figure this thing out. I mean, I know there's a God. And I know I'm supposed to act a certain way and everything. But to be real, babe, I'm still researching this whole salvation thing." He tilted his head. "I mean, I don't wanna just dive into it without understanding what it's all about, if that makes any sense."

Vanessa nodded. "It make perfect sense, baby. I get it."

"I will say this, though. I felt really good when I was in church today."

She smiled. "Yeah?"

"Yeah, it felt like everything was finally moving in the right direction, you know? Like I was exactly where I was supposed to be." His eyebrows furrowed. "But, then there's the parts that I can't figure out. Like, if God is all-loving and all-seeing, why does He allow things like rape, murder, war?"

She studied him with a smile. "You've really been giving this a lot of thought."

"Well, yeah. Just the other night was I watching this Muslim speaker on TV and he was talking about the book that they read—the Koran," he said. "And, basically, Muslims believe that Jesus existed, but that He was only a prophet. Not the Son of God. And he gave a bunch of scientific facts to back up everything he was saying."

"How did that make you feel?" she asked.

"I don't know. I thought it was interesting, I guess." He shrugged. "To be honest, V. It's just a lot to swallow."

"Well, whenever you're ready," she caressed the back of his neck, "whenever you're ready…hopefully sooner rather than later," she added, grinning, "just know that I'm here if you ever want to talk about it."

"I know," he said, smiling as he leaned in and thanked her with a kiss.

20

"I hope you brought your appetites," Caesar Montego said. "Because your mother cooks enough for an army." Miles' dad was an amiable man with a deep voice and a commanding presence. Thanking him as he poured her a glass of wine, Vanessa marveled at the resemblance between father and son.

Ever the hostess, Julia Montego bustled from the kitchen with a freshly tossed salad and warm, oven-baked rolls.

"It looks good, Ma," Miles said. She'd cooked all of his favorites and, in honor of Vanessa, had set up a beautiful spread on the back patio, replete with a floral centerpiece and the sterling silver flatware that she only brought out for special occasions.

"I'll be right back with the soup," Julia said, already making her way toward the house again.

"Lemme give you a hand." Pushing his chair from the table, Miles followed his mother inside, where he found her ladling lobster bisque into four bowls.

"Almost done in here," she said, garnishing each serving with a few sprigs of parsley. "Whoo!" Julia dabbed her forehead with a nearby dishtowel and steadied herself against one of the counters.

"You okay, Ma?"

She dismissed his concerns with a few hurried waves of her hand. "I'm fine. Just a little tired."

His mother had always been naturally slim with lithe limbs that made her mannerisms look regal, graceful, no matter how mundane the activity. But as he observed her while she moved around the spacious kitchen, he noticed that her posture was strained, her movements uncharacteristically languid. Dark circles framed her usually bright eyes and her face, once soft and full, looked gaunt and leathery.

Pouring the remainder of the soup into a porcelain serving dish, Julia wiped down the stovetop and started to move the dirty pot to the sink, but was stopped by a coughing fit that shook her slight frame. Julia covered her mouth and turned her head in an attempt to avoid Miles' probing gaze.

"You sure you're all right, Ma," he asked, drawing near. He placed the back of his hand against her forehead. "It sounds like you might be coming down with a cold."

"Oh, stop it." She shooed him away. "If you want something to fuss over, here, take these to the table." She handed him the bowls of steaming soup. "I'm right behind you."

Despite his reservations, he obeyed and rejoined his dad and Vanessa on the patio.

"Mmmmm!" Vanessa smiled as Miles served the bisque. "That smells delicious."

Caesar nodded. "Tastes even better," he promised.

Julia emerged from the house moments later wearing a fresh coat of lipstick. "Everyone all set?" she asked, taking her seat beside her husband.

Vanessa eyed the spread in front of them. "Mrs. Montego, you really outdid yourself."

"Well, I had to pull out all the stops for the woman who got my son to go to church!"

Caesar raised a skeptical brow. "You got Miles to go to church?"

Vanessa nodded. "This past Sunday."

"I don't believe it!" he teased.

"That's what I said." Julia grinned. "Vanessa, you're a miracle worker! You just don't know how hard I've been praying for this boy."

"Well, that makes two of us," Vanessa said.

They all laughed.

"All right, all right. Let's bless this food before it gets cold," Julia said. She and Caesar bowed their heads. Holding hands, Vanessa and Miles followed suit.

"Dear Lord," Julia began. "Thank You for the food we are about to receive for the nourishment and health of our bodies. Thank You for our wonderful son, Miles. And for bringing the beautiful Vanessa into our lives. She is truly an angel from heaven. In Jesus' name we pray. Amen."

"Amen," the rest of them echoed.

Caesar placed his napkin in his lap. "Now, Vanessa, honey. Don't be afraid to crack the whip on this young man, here," he said, pointing at Miles.

"That's right." Julia's nod was decisive. "And if he gives you any trouble, you just let us know. We'll straighten him out."

"I like the sound of that," Vanessa said, smiling as Miles shook his head with feigned disapproval.

The mood was jovial as they dug into their meal. Vanessa enjoyed listening to Mrs. Montego's stories about Miles' childhood and talking with Mr. Montego about everything from classic cars to the latest exhibits at the San Jose Museum of Art.

By the time they'd cleared the table and gone inside for dessert and coffee, Caesar and Julia Montego felt like Vanessa was already part of the family.

"You've got your hands full with that one," Julia told Vanessa as they scraped the remnants of their dinner into the trashcan and loaded the dirty plates into the dishwasher. "But you're doing a great job."

From the pass through in the kitchen, Vanessa watched Miles and his dad laugh as they slowly flipped through an old photo album. She smiled. "It's not hard. He's easy to love."

"More so since you've been around. I can't remember a time when I saw him this happy, this carefree. You're good for him."

Vanessa shrugged. "We're good for each other."

"Well, I'm just glad we finally got to—" Her sentence was cut off by the sound of wine glasses crashing against the tile floor. When Vanessa looked up, a winded Julia was trying to catch her breath.

"Mrs. Montego, are you okay?" Vanessa asked, rushing to her side.

Miles called from the living room. "Everything all right in there?"

"We're fine," Julia tried to call back. The words came out as a breathy wheeze. She looked to Vanessa for help.

"Yeah, we're fine," she said. "Just a couple of butterfingers."

Vanessa helped Julia to one of the nearby barstools and sat with her until the episode passed. "Are you sure you don't want me to get Mr. Montego for you?" she asked, as Julia took the final few sips of the glass of water Vanessa had fetched her.

"No. I'm all better now." She smiled. "No need to cause a panic over a bit of indigestion, right?"

"Well, is there anything else you need?"

"I think I can handle the rest of the dishes," she said standing. "Why don't you head on out there with the cake and coffee. I'm right behind you."

Vanessa tried to protest, but Miles' mom would hear none of it. Reluctantly, Vanessa joined Miles and Caesar in the next room as Julia Montego grabbed a dustpan and began sweeping shards of glass from the floor.

21

Agent Jason McDaniel sat back with a sigh as he surveyed the most recent surveillance video of Miles Montego and his crew. For the past several weeks, he'd made a point of holing up in one of the empty conference rooms at the end of the day, long after the last computer had been powered down and all of the agents had returned to their families and their lives. He spent hours, sometimes through the night and early into the next morning, combing through stacks of files and scrutinizing hours of stakeout footage, trying to find a clue—to pinpoint that one solid lead that would blow open the whole investigation.

The task force that Agent Edgemond formed had put its heart and soul into building the strongest case possible. His men had gone to great lengths to gain insight into all of the members. They'd tapped phones and dug through trash. They'd investigated their friends and families, researched their hangouts and habits. They'd learned their routines and memorized their behaviors. And they'd taken all of the facts, from the significant to the seemingly inconsequential, catalogued them and filed them away with the expectation that they would eventually fit together like pieces of an intricate puzzle.

Over the better part of a year, the team had gathered a lot of good evidence on Martin, Chris, Wikki, and Percy—enough to put them away for a very long time. But for all their hard work and thorough sleuthing, they hadn't yet dug up any dirt on Montego.

McDaniel studied the images of Miles playing on the projection screen in front of him. They had hours of footage of him running innocuous errands, hanging around town with his new lady friend and visiting his parents. But unlike his counterparts, who made a habit of meeting up with known drug dealers in out of the way locations and exchanging large amounts of drugs for even larger amounts of cash, Miles was clean. All the leads they'd followed up on, including the mysterious T, had been dead ends. And to top it off, Miles appeared to be spending less time at his regular haunts and more and more time at church, of all places.

He leaned forward and shook his head. "How come I can't figure out who you really are?" he murmured.

Like all seasoned DEA vets, McDaniel had developed an intimate knowledge of how drug crews operated—how they thought, the way they talked and moved. But never in his years as an agent had he run across a God-fearing kingpin.

"I see you're working late again," a familiar voice said. Terry Edgemond took the seat beside him.

McDaniel nodded, his eyes still trained on the video ahead. "I told you we're gonna nail these guys, right? So, if they're working late..."

"We gotta be working late," Edgemond concluded.

"Exactly." McDaniel scribbled a few notes on the pad in his lap as new footage of Miles talking outside at night on his cell phone flickered across the screen. "Still nothing on him yet," McDaniel said, motioning toward the images of Miles. "I can't seem to crack him."

"He'll slip up eventually," Edgemond said. "They always do."

"I don't know. He's not like the others."

"If there's something there, you'll find it." Agent Edgemond's tone was confident, his nod resolute.

"Yes, sir," he said. But as Edgemond gathered his briefcase and headed for the door, McDaniel couldn't help but wonder if just maybe, there was nothing there to find.

22

"Vanessa, it was so nice meeting your family today," Caesar said, settling into the living room sofa beside Julia. Miles and Vanessa sat across from them, both nursing glasses of eggnog. In the corner, a Christmas tree glowed with twinkling lights and beneath it several gifts sat unopened.

"You're all so beautiful," Julia added.

Caesar chuckled. "With such pretty daughters, it's no wonder your father turned to the Lord. That man must spend a lot of time on his knees."

Vanessa nodded and raised her glass in the air. "Amen!"

They all laughed.

Miles had spent his Christmas day with the Leons, opening presents, meeting their very large, very loud extended family, and gorging himself on a delicious dinner feast, all while dodging Lydia's scathing gazes. Afterward the two families met for the first time at an evening service at the Leons' church, where they enjoyed a time of fellowship and praise, and Pastor Tim gave an inspired sermon about the real meaning of the Christmas.

It had been a long, busy day, but Miles and Vanessa had made the trek to his parents' house in order to exchange gifts.

Julia braced her hand on her chest as she was attacked by yet another coughing fit. They were wet and phlegmy and had hit her at regular intervals all evening. At times, the episodes were so forceful that it sounded as though she'd rattled loose a lung.

Miles frowned. "Ma, I told you last time I saw you to get that cough checked out."

She took a sip of her hot tea. "And I told you it's nothing but a harmless cold."

Miles looked to his father for backup, but he just shrugged. "You know your mother, Son. She thinks everything can be cured with an aspirin."

"Well, it can't." He glanced at his mom as she tried to muffle another cough with her handkerchief. "And now a simple cold might've turned into bronchitis or worse, pneumonia."

Julia shook her head. "You're such an alarmist, Miles. Honestly, it's nothing," she said. "Now, come on. Let's open some presents. Hand me that one Caesar." She pointed to a festive looking bag under the Christmas tree. "Vanessa, honey, this one is from me."

"Thank you!" Vanessa shot Miles a questioning look, but he appeared just as eager as she to see what was inside.

Delicately, Vanessa removed the decorative tissue paper and fished out a heavy wooden box. When she unfastened the latch and looked inside, she discovered an ornate Fabergé egg nested inside. Her eyes widened. "It's gorgeous!"

Julia smiled. "A little birdie mentioned that you collect them."

In her room, Vanessa kept six beautifully decorated eggs prominently displayed on her bookcase. They'd been given to her, over the years, by different family members.

She'd taken a liking to the jeweled treasures as a child while visiting an Imperial Fabergé exhibit at the San Jose Museum of Art. Their baroque design and elaborate detail fascinated her, as did their worth and rarity. But most of all she'd fallen in love with the story behind them. The idea that something that timeless, that exquisite had been commissioned by a husband as a gift for his wife seemed impossibly romantic and made her long for the day when she would grow up and find a prince charming of her own.

That same year, Vanessa's parents purchased her a lovely Fabergé replica for her birthday. And the following Easter, one of her aunts did the same. Slowly, her collection of eggs grew, but none of them came close this beauty.

"It was my mother's," Julia said, smiling as Vanessa admired the keepsake. "And my mother's mother before that."

"Mrs. Montego, this is too much," Vanessa said.

"Nonsense." Julia stifled another cough. "It was handed down to me and I always thought someday I'd pass it on to my child; but that one," she said, motioning toward Miles, "doesn't know the difference between a Fabergé egg and a scrambled one."

Miles laughed. "Thanks. I think."

"Yeah, but don't you want to keep it?" Vanessa asked, running her fingers across the gold latticework. "Enjoy it a little longer?"

"If there's one thing I've learned at my age, it's that you should never put off for later what you can do today. And things like this are meant to be shared. Besides," she shrugged, "I can't take it with me, right?"

"Take it with you? Ma, you make it sound like you're an old lady or something." Miles smirked. "You're gonna be around for many years to come."

"That's the plan, anyway," she said.

Vanessa thought back to the evening Julia collapsed on the kitchen floor. Her stomach churned uneasily.

Miles nodded. "That's more like it."

Vanessa hugged the box close. "Thank you, Mrs. Montego," she said, blinking back tears. "I will cherish it always."

Her smile was meaningful. "I know you will."

"Okay." Miles rubbed his hands together and retrieved a large white envelope topped with a bow. "Now it's our turn." He and Vanessa smiled as he handed his father the packet. "We know y'all been trying to get away for some time. So we got you a little something we think you'll like."

"Now wait a minute, Son," Caesar said. "What is this?"

"Open it."

Julia did the honors. When she saw the brochure for Sandals Resorts and two first-class tickets to the Bahamas, she started to scream. "Caesar, baby. Look at this place!" she said, flipping feverishly through the glossy catalog.

His father smiled. "Son, this is beautiful, but you shouldn't have."

"Ah, come on, Pop. You two been wanting to go on vacation for years. This is our gift to you."

"Oooo, it's just like the commercial," Julia said, still looking at the colorful photos.

"Now, Ma. Ma." Miles motioned for her to calm down and listen. "There is one condition," he said.

Julia's brows furrowed. "And what's that?"

"You gotta promise me you're gonna see a doctor about that cough. Soon."

"Oh, Miles. Please." She rolled her eyes.

Calling her bluff, Miles took back the brochure and tickets and returned them to the envelope. "No doctor, no trip," he said.

It was Julia's turn to look to Caesar for backup. Again, he just shrugged. "The man drives a hard bargain."

"All right, fine. Whatever. I promise."

Miles smiled. "Thank you, Ma."

"No, thank *you*—both of you," she said, giving Vanessa a hug and then pulling Miles in for a long embrace. "I couldn't have asked for a better son or a fuller life." Julia blinked back the mist in her eyes. "I can die a happy woman, now."

"Merry Christmas, Ma," Miles said, holding her close. "I love you."

"I love you, too, baby. To the ends of the earth and back."

Miles chuckled, a sense of nostalgia washing over him. It was something they use to tell each other every night after she'd tucked him in to bed. "And forever and a day," he said.

A single tear slid down her check as she smiled, "And into eternity."

23

The night had started as a quiet evening in. Half-empty Chinese cartons sat on the coffee table, *Love & Basketball* played on the plasma screen hanging from the wall, and Miles and Vanessa sat snuggled close on the couch in his living room, their feet hidden beneath a woolly blanket.

Maybe it was the dim light and the softly glowing candles. Maybe it was the scent of Miles' cologne or the way his shirt showed off his muscular biceps. Or maybe it was the extra glass of wine she'd had at dinner. But she was maddeningly aware of the undeniable attraction between them.

Miles felt the same way and had worked hard all evening to avoid ogling her toned legs—put on full display by a pair of cutoff shorts—or peek at the small amounts of cleavage revealed by her V-neck sweater every time she bent forward to take a sip of her drink.

They'd been together for nearly a year and he'd been faithful to her, in every sense of the word. It was a great feeling being committed to someone who was just as dedicated to him as he was to her. And over the months Vanessa had come to provide a certain sense of security, stability. But he'd learned early on in their relationship that security and stability came with a heavy price tag, namely celibacy.

He'd messed with plenty of women who'd claimed to follow a certain code of conduct when it came to sex. There was the "Third Date Rule," the "One Month Rule," the "90-Day Rule"—he'd been up against them all, and won. But Vanessa had made it abundantly clear that she had no plans to get physical with him or anyone else for that matter until her wedding night.

It was a stance that he found admirable and frustrating in equal measure. He wanted to respect her wishes—even if they were a little dated for his tastes—but, she was so beautiful and he loved her so much that lately he'd had a hard time keeping his hands off her.

Usually she rebuffed his advances. But tonight she didn't resist when he slid her close and draped her legs over his. Or when he snaked his arm around her tiny waist and rested his hand against the curve of her hip. And when his tender kisses grew more passionate, more insistent, instead of pulling away and telling him to stop, she leaned into his embrace.

He grew increasingly eager as he caressed her smooth calf, allowing his hand to inch past her knee to her thigh. Reflexively, Vanessa's back arched and a soft moan escaped her lips. With quickening breaths, she ran her fingers along his chest and around his shoulders.

Hurriedly, Miles laid her down on the sofa. As he nibbled on her ear then kissed her jaw, his hand found its way beneath her sweater and fumbled for the clasp of her bra.

"Babe," she turned her face, "I can't."

"Don't say that," he whispered, reaching once more beneath her sweater.

"No." This time her voice was forceful, her tone resolute. She pushed him away and sat up. "We can't."

Miles flopped against the cushions with a fed-up sigh and rubbed his head. "Why not?"

"You know why," Vanessa said, pulling her legs to her chest and resting her chin on her knees. "We've talk about this."

"But it doesn't make any sense," he argued. "This isn't some cheap fling, some sleazy one-night stand. We're two adults in a committed relationship. I love you."

She nodded. "And I love you."

"So then what's the problem?" he asked, holding his arms out helplessly. "V, I want you. I'm not ashamed to admit it. Sex is the highest expression of love between two people. I want that with you, for us."

"I want that for us too, baby, but not before we're married. Not before it's been ordained by God."

Miles wagged his finger in the air as though what she'd said reminded him of something. Turning from his seat on the sofa, he reached for his Bible on the side table behind him and flipped to a tabbed section in Song of Solomon. "Listen to this. 'How much more pleasing is your love than wine,'" he began, his voice theatrically low. "'Your lips drop sweetness as the honeycomb, my bride; milk and honey are under your tongue.'"

Smirking, Vanessa stifled a giggle.

"'Listen, my love is knocking. My head is drenched with dew. I've taken off my robe, must I put it on again? My beloved thrust his hand into the opening and my inmost being yearned for him. I arose to open to my beloved..." Miles closed the Bible and shrugged as though he'd just made an open and shut case. "Sounds like late-night Cinemax to me."

Vanessa laughed. "Hold up," she said, shaking her head. "If you could've heard how you just read that."

"What? I was just reading..." He pointed to the Book in his lap. "That's what it says."

Tilting her head, Vanessa's studied him appraisingly. "Babe. Are you trying to suggest that the Bible says it's okay for us to have sex?"

He shook his head, feeling suddenly foolish and awkward. "I don't know what the Bible is saying, V. I'm just trying to figure it out."

She nodded. "Okay. Well, I can almost assure you that the people in those passages are married. I mean, making love in itself isn't a sin. The Bible says that you can totally enjoy your spouse sexually, you know?"

He tossed the Bible on the coffee table with a shrug.

"How did you interpret it?" she asked.

"Just forget it." He stood, his face hot. "I'm sorry I even brought it up."

"No, baby. This is good. It's important that we're able to discuss these things."

"Drop it," he said, crossing the room in three angry strides.

"Miles," Vanessa called after him. "Are you serious?"

But all she heard in response was the sound of his heavy footsteps heading upstairs, followed by the sharp slam of his bedroom door.

24

"Miles, my man! What's up, baby?" Martin joined Miles at the bar, where he was brooding alone, nursing a double shot of Courvoisier. It was a typical Saturday night at their favorite club. The music was loud, the atmosphere hype. And all around him people were drinking, talking, laughing, and dancing.

"Marty, what's up," Miles said, giving him a handshake and a hug.

"Where you been at, man? I haven't see you around in a minute."

Miles shrugged. "Rippin' and runnin', baby. Just rippin' and runnin'."

"You all right, Miles?"

"Don't I look all right?" Miles finished the rest of his drink in one swallow. "Hey," he called to the bartender a few feet away. "Lemme get another one."

Martin's studied him for a moment, his gaze probing. "Yo, where's Vanessa?"

"I don't know." Turning around, Miles leaned back and rested his elbows on the bar. "She's around somewhere. Just not here with me, ya know?"

The truth was, he hadn't seen Vanessa in almost a week. Even though he missed her and she'd called him countless times, he couldn't bring himself to face her after she'd shot him down again. He'd changed a lot since they'd been together. He'd given up a lot of the things and the people who had once characterized him. But it was never enough.

No matter how hard he tried to be that perfect, God-fearing man she wanted, he always seemed to come up short.

Martin nudged him. "So then you ready to party with your boys tonight?"

"You know what?" Miles stood up straight, and feeling a surge of his old adrenaline, tugged at the edges of his leather jacket. "Let's do that. I ain't been with y'all in a minute," he said. "Let's do what we do. Drinks are on me tonight."

"That's what I'm talking about," Martin said, wrapping an arm around Miles' shoulder. "The man is back!" Together they made their way to a VIP table where the rest of the crew were clowning and having a good time.

"Aye, look who it is," Percy said, when he saw Martin approaching with Miles.

Wikki smiled. "Now it's a party for real!"

Miles and Martin took a seat as the waitress delivered another round of drinks.

"Keep 'em coming all night, beautiful," Chris said, pounding back his shot.

Laughing, Miles did the same.

"Yo, Miles. So what's going on with you man, for real?" Martin asked, leaning in so he could be heard above the pulsing music.

Miles shrugged. "With what?"

"With you, homie. I mean, we don't ever see you around no more, Dogg. And when we do, it's never without Vanessa."

"Yeah, and?" Miles sat back. "What's your point?"

Martin put his hands up in a show of amity. "Look, man. Me and you, we go way back—longer than any of these cats right here," he said, motioning toward the rest of the group. "We been through a lot, you know what I'm saying? And I ain't never seen you knocked off your square by a girl. So if you need to talk about it, for real, I'm right here like I always been. I'm all ears." He shrugged. "But if not, that's cool too."

"Thanks, man. I appreciate it." Miles said, nodding. "Really, though, I'm good. I just got a lot going on right now, that's all."

Martin smirked. "Well, then, I got just what you need to take your mind of things. Aye, yo, ladies!" he said, calling over a lingering clique of beautiful women. "Come on in here. Let's get this thing started."

Stepping aside, the bouncer controlling the traffic in and out of the VIP section granted them entry. The women, all scantily clad and ready to party, made themselves comfortable among the crew. A tall Latina wearing a clinging mini dress with a neck line that plunged to her navel chose the seat beside Miles. She introduced herself as Kiana.

Her thick hair fell like a curtain against his back as she leaned in and whispered into his ear. "I've been waiting all night to talk to you."

She smelled like cheap perfume and booze. "Oh, yeah?" he asked, putting a little space between them as he reached for his glass.

Nodding, she scooted closer. "You're sexy," she said, her breath hot against his cheek.

Miles' smile was polite, his tone disinterested. "Thank you."

She moved even closer. "What do you say we find a quieter spot to talk?"

Miles looked at the circle of friends seated around him. Decked out in designer threads and custom jewelry, drinks in their hands, pretty girls hanging on them—they were in their element. This is who they'd always been and, quite possibly, who they would always choose to be, but he couldn't say the same for himself. Things were different now. This wasn't where he belonged anymore.

Still, for reasons he couldn't explain, Miles didn't resist when Kiana grabbed his hand and brazenly led him to an empty couch at the back of the lounge.

~

Outside, Vanessa pulled in front of the nightclub's entrance. On her way home from dinner with girlfriends she couldn't resist the urge to swing by and see if Miles was there.

She hated the fact that it had come to this. That instead of facing their problems head-on and working through them like adults, she'd been forced to resort to sneaky drive-bys just to have a conversation with her boyfriend. But all of her attempts to talk about what had happened were shrugged off. And in the past couple of days, he'd managed to avoid her altogether.

Vanessa's pulse quickened as she spotted Miles' black Bentley parked in the valet line along the curb. Turning on her emergency lights, she pulled into a nearby loading zone and rushed inside.

It was dark and loud as she maneuvered her way through the dense crowd of people. She scanned the bar and then surveyed the mass of bodies on the dance floor. But Miles was nowhere to be found. Turning around, Vanessa doubled back and headed for the VIP lounge. She heard Martin's laughter before she ever saw him and the rest of the guys seated with a group of girls she didn't recognize. A mounting sense of dread was settling in the pit of her stomach as she combed the rest of the room.

And then she spotted him. Slouched on a couch in the back with a drink in his hand and girl draped over his shoulder.

Hot tears instantly sprang to Vanessa's eyes as she watched the woman rub his chest and whisper into his ear. He said something back and the woman smiled. Taking the glass from his hand, she placed it on the table in front of them. Then with a flirtatious caress of his face, she turned his head so that their lips were just inches apart and leaned in for a kiss.

Vanessa turned away, unable to watch, and dashed toward the exit. Her tears fell freely as she pushed her way through the crowd of late night partiers and into the cool night air. Ignoring the stares from curious strangers, she stumbled to her car, got in, and collapsed against the steering wheel with heaving sobs.

25

According to the clock on Miles' nightstand, it was 1:30 in the morning when he finally walked into his room and kicked off his shoes. He hung up his jacket, tossed his pants in the hamper, and headed straight for the shower.

Miles was in no particular rush as he leaned into the hot spray and breathed the steam into his lungs. The water pelted his skin, washing away the day's worries and relaxed his tense muscles.

He regretted going to the club tonight. He regretted making such a big deal about sex with Vanessa. He regretted ignoring her calls. He regretted everything. Sitting in that lounge with a strange woman's hands all over him and a voice that wasn't Vanessa's in his ear made him feel like a stranger in his own skin.

He'd turn away when Kiana had tried to kiss him, told her he was taken and left her stunned, confused, and alone on the couch. When Martin saw him making a beeline for the door, he tried to convince him to stay. Said they were taking the party to his house and promised Miles a wild and crazy night, just like the old days. But Miles passed, uninterested in going back to the man he used to be.

Turning off the water, Miles stepped out of the shower and grabbed a towel. He dried himself off then slipped into a wife beater and a pair lounge pants and climbed into bed with a tired sigh. As he grabbed the remote control and reached to turn off the lamp, he noticed the voicemail indicator flashing on his cell phone. Miles punched in his passcode and listened to the first of several messages waiting for him.

"Miles, it's me," Vanessa's voice, hoarse and quaking, filtered through the receiver. "I was there tonight. I saw you…with her." He sat up, instantly alarmed.

"How could you do this, Miles? Why?" Vanessa asked, choking back a sob. "I thought you were different. You seemed so different." She sniffled. "I guess that was my mistake."

He hung up, not bothering to listen to any of the other messages and, heart pounding, dialed Vanessa's number.

"What do you want, Miles," she asked in lieu of "Hello." She sounded cold and eerily detached.

"Baby, let me explain."

"I'm not interested in anything you have to say."

"V, it's not what it looked like. You gotta believe me."

"Well, I don't," she said, her volume rising.

"Nothing happened!"

Vanessa's chortle was caustic. "Don't treat me like I'm stupid, Miles. I know what I saw!" she shouted.

"Baby, I know it looked bad, okay? I can't imagine…if I—if the shoe was on the other foot, I don't know what I would've done."

"How do you expect me to trust you again?" she asked, sounding betrayed, defeated. "I feel like I don't even know who you are."

"Don't say that, V. Please, don't say that."

"I gotta go, Miles."

"Wait. Baby, don't hang up. We need to talk. When can I see you?" he asked. But it was too late. She was gone.

Miles dialed her number again. This time the call went straight to voicemail. Desperate to clear things up, he headed to his closet to change. As he tugged on a pair of jeans and a sweatshirt, he mentally rehearsed what he would say in the very likely event that one of Vanessa's parents answered when he rang the doorbell. He imagined Lydia's contemptuous expression at the sight of him on her front porch at three in the morning.

"Mr. and Mrs. Leon," he practiced aloud as he pulled on a pair of socks. "I'm sorry to disturb you at the hour, but I need to speak with Vanessa. It's an emergency."

Of course, they would want to know what the emergency was, he reasoned. Lacing up his sneakers, Miles tried to think of a believable story, but nothing came to mind. By the time he stuffed his wallet into his back pocket and grabbed his keys from off his dresser, he'd decided that his best bet would be to tell the truth and let the chips fall where they may.

Bounding down the stairs, two at a time, he reached the front door just as his phone rang. He didn't recognize the number that flashed on the screen. "Hello?" he answered, hoping to her Vanessa's voice on the other end.

"Miles?"

"Pop?"

"Son, where've you been? I've been trying to reach you all night."

"I'm sorry." Miles glanced at the voicemail indicator still flashing on his phone. "I just got home. Is everything okay?"

"No," he said. "I'm at Regional Medical Center."

"Why? What's wrong?"

"It's your mother, Miles. She's sick—very sick. I need you to get down here as soon as you possibly can."

26

The lobby of RMC was empty, save for a security guard standing post just inside the automatic doors and two women, dressed in matching scrubs stationed at the guest services desk. "Yes, sir. Can I help you?" the one seated behind the computer asked.

"My mom. I got a call. She was brought here by ambulance," he said, barely able to string together a complete thought.

"Do you know what ward she's in?"

Miles shook his head.

"Well, what was she brought in for?"

"I don't know." His voice was pitched high with worry and impatience. "My dad. He just called and told me to rush down here. I have no idea what's going on."

"Okay, no problem," she said calmly, slowly. "What's your mom's name? I can look her up in the system."

"Julia Montego." He watched anxiously as her fingers danced across the keyboard in front her. "Here we go. It looks like she was just moved to room 2204." She handed Miles a visitor's badge. "The elevators are around the corner, to your left," she said. "Take them up to the second floor and follow the corridor all the way around. She'll be in the fourth room on the right."

Thanking her, Miles rushed to the row of elevators and tried not to think the worst as he stepped on and took the short ride up. The squeak of his soles against the shiny linoleum floors was the only sound in the deserted hallway as he made his way around a bend and to a set of partition doors that led to the Critical Care Unit.

Miles found his mom lying in a narrow bed. All around her machines beeped, monitoring her vitals as a coiled IV line pumped fluids into a vein in her arm and a nasal cannula, wrapped around her ears and inserted into her nostrils fed oxygen to her lungs. Her body looked frail, her skin pallid against the sterile white sheets.

"Thank God you're here, Son," Caesar said, startling Miles when he entered the room. He turned to see his father seated in a chair in the corner, a weathered expression on his face.

"I'm sorry, Pop. I got here as soon as I could." He sat gently on the edge of the bed and held his mother's hand. "How's she doing?"

Before his dad could answer, Miles' mom opened her eyes. "I'll be just fine," she said, her smile weak. "I told you not to fuss so much."

He chuckled. "I can't help it, Ma. I'm your son. It's what I do."

"I'm sorry I ruined the trip, baby." She turned her head and coughed. "Such a shame."

"Trip?" Miles shook his head. "Ma, don't even worry about that. The only thing I want you to concentrate on is getting better, you hear me?"

She nodded groggily before closing her eyes and drifting off to sleep.

"She's heavily sedated," his father explained.

"Well, what's wrong? What did the doctor say?"

His mother stirred languidly.

"Let's talk outside," Caesar suggested. "So she can rest."

Miles followed his dad to an adjacent waiting room. An infomercial played quietly on a mounted television in the corner. They chose two chairs away from the handful of people scattered across the bank of blue, plastic chairs.

Miles wasted no time. "What's wrong with her?"

"Your mother's been diagnosed with cancer," his father said. "It's bad, Son. Stage 4."

"I don't understand. Can't they give her something?

Caesar shook his head. "It's too late for that. Her heart's just not strong enough to pump blood to her body."

"Well what about surgery?" Miles asked. "A bypass or a transplant."

"Maybe. If we'd caught it earlier, but the fact is she's too weak. She wouldn't survive any of the procedures available to her."

Miles' eyes filled with tears. "I don't understand. How does someone go from being perfectly healthy to dying overnight?"

"It wasn't overnight, Son. Apparently, she's been living with this for years. But you know your mother and doctors." He shrugged. "We had no way of knowing until now."

"So, what next?"

"The goal is to keep her as comfortable as possible," his father explained. "She's got fluid in lungs, her liver's failing and her kidneys are shutting down. She's suffering, Miles."

"How much longer?"

"Maybe a day or two. A week at the most."

"Son, listen to me." He watched as Miles wiped his tears on his sleeve. "Right now, I need you to be strong. For your mother. Okay?"

"Yeah, Pop."

"Good," Caesar said, giving him a hug. "That's my boy."

27

Miles and his father spent the next few days camped out at his mother's side. A constant rotation of orderlies, nurses, doctors, and specialists tramped in and out of her room several times an hour, changing IV bags, resetting machines, checking vital signs, and drawing blood. His mother, who seemed impervious to it all, barely moved unless it was to cough or request ice chips.

There was nothing he could do to make it better, no amount of money he could pay could fix it. He couldn't pull strings or call in favors. He couldn't do anything but sit and wait for his mother's body to slowly and painfully shut down.

A couple of the nurses had suggested that he go home, change clothes, get some sleep. Even his father, who had left to shower and eat a decent meal, begged Miles to take a break. But he couldn't bring himself to leave her side, didn't want to risk the chance of walking away and missing his chance to say goodbye.

"Knock, knock." Judy, one of the dayshift nurses rapped on the door. She was young with a round face and a cheery disposition. "Just want to get a quick blood pressure reading."

Miles nodded. "Do your thing."

She rolled the machine to his mother's beside and fastened the cuff around her arm. "How's she doing with pain?" Judy asked, as she pressed a few buttons and the cuff began to inflate.

"Okay, I guess." Miles shrugged. "I mean, she hasn't complained again since they set up the morphine drip."

"Good." The machine beeped, prompting Judy to scribble a few notes on his mother's chart. She removed the cuff and rolled the machine back into the corner.

"How is it?" Miles asked

"Low," she said with a sympathetic tilt of her head. "But that's to be expected."

Miles rubbed his face and sighed.

"Are you absolutely sure I can't get you anything, Mr. Montego?"

"No. I'm good." He nodded his appreciation. "Thank you, though."

Judy left just as his father entered carrying a Styrofoam cup of coffee and a copy of the *San Jose Mercury* under his arm. "You'll never guess who I ran into downstairs."

Miles rubbed his tired eyes. "Who, Pop?"

"Me," Vanessa said, stepping into the room behind Caesar.

"V." Miles stood up. His posture was stiff, his gaze uncertain. "What're you doing here?"

"I called her," Caesar said matter-of-factly. "I don't know what's going on between you two and I don't need to know." He glanced tenderly at Julia sleeping nearby. "I'll just say this—if there's one thing I've learned in forty-six years of marriage it's that you have to love the one you're with as true as you can, as best as you can, for as long as you can. Because tomorrow's never promised. And forever is never as far away as it seems."

Miles watched his dad pull a chair beside his mother and greet her with a gentle kiss on the back of her hand. Her eyes fluttered open and, at the sight of him, her expression brightened.

"Can we talk?" Vanessa asked.

Miles looked back at his mom, torn between leaving and staying.

"Oh, go on," his dad said, shooing them away with a nod of his head. "Give an old man a few minutes alone with the love of his life." Julia chuckled and reached out her hand to touch Caesar's face.

Despite himself, Miles smiled and followed Vanessa into the ICU waiting room.

"Miles, I'm so sorry," Vanessa said, sitting down beside him. Tentatively, she touched his arm. "I can't even imagine what you're going through right now."

"Babe, I need to explain what happened."

"You don't have to explain anything."

"Yes, I do," he insisted. "I mean, I know it's probably not the right time—"

She shook her head. "It's not the right time."

"V, please. Just listen to me! I don't know what's going on inside. I've never experienced these sort of emotions before." Sighing, he searched for the words. "It's like I'm feeling anger, guilt, and shame all at once. Sometimes, I don't feel like I deserve anything and then other times I get confused about what God is telling me. I just...I'm never sure if I'm doing the right thing anymore." Turning to face her, Miles tilted Vanessa's chin upward until their eyes met. "But I want you to understand something. I want you to know that absolutely nothing happened the other night."

"Miles, you don't have to..."

"Vanessa, I love you," he said, holding her gaze. There was a pleading in his voice she'd never heard before. "I love you, and I would never, ever do anything to hurt you."

She cupped the side of his face in her hand. "Is that the whole truth, Miles?"

"Baby, ain't no question," he said, resting his head on her shoulder and heaving a sigh of relief as she whispered into his ears the three words he'd been desperately waiting to hear.

"I believe you."

~

When Mrs. Montego requested to speak with her privately, Vanessa could barely hold her composure. Julia patted a spot on the mattress and motioned for Vanessa to sit beside her. "Vanessa, baby. I need you to do something for me."

"Anything you ask me to do, I'll do it," Vanessa said, her petite frame shuddering with a fresh waves of tears.

"Don't cry, just listen." Julia squeezed her hand. "I need you to take care of Miles for me. I know there's a reason why you two met. God knew that the only way He could capture Miles' heart was through someone like you—a beautiful, wonderful, godly woman." She smiled. "Please don't ever give up on him. If you really love him."

"I do," Vanessa said, nodding as she was choking back a sob. "I really do."

"Good. Then, I want a big wedding and a lot of grandbabies, you hear me?"

"Please don't talk like that Mrs. Montego. You're gonna be fine."

"No, honey, I'm not," she said, holding her chest as she coughed. Julia took a moment to steady her breathing before she continued. "I need you and Miles to keep seeking the Lord together. And always remember, that He is the answer to all of your problems. He has big plans for you two. Big plans—" Turning her head, she covered her mouth and coughed again. It was a loud, guttural hack that shook her body violently.

When she moved her hand, her palm was covered with blood.

Vanessa stood, panicked. "Somebody!" she screamed, as the machines in the room began to alarm. Julia gurgled and a pink foam bubbled up from her throat and dribbled down her chin. "Somebody, please help!"

Miles was by her side in an instant, followed by several nurses.

"I don't know what happened," Vanessa said, backing away.

"She can't breathe!" Miles looked around at the huddle of hospital staff watching his mother struggle to stay alive. "Do something!" he shouted angrily.

"They can't," his father said, rushing to his wife's side.

"What do you mean they can't?" Miles glared at the nurses as they turned off several of the monitors. "Why are you just standing there?" he bellowed.

"Son, please. It's okay. Your mother asked not to be resuscitated. She doesn't want to live like this. She doesn't want to suffer any longer than she has to."

Lying down beside his wife, Caesar held her in his arms. "I'm here, sweetheart," he said, rocking her gently as he stroked her hair. "It's okay. I'm here."

Gradually, Julia stopped struggling. Her labored breathing slowed and her muscles relaxed. "That's it," Caesar soothed. Miles watched helplessly as his father kissed her temple. "Go in peace, my love," he whispered.

And with his blessing, she closed her eyes and crossed into eternity.

28

A light drizzle fell as Agent McDaniel and Agent Stokes staked out Julia Montego's funeral from their surveillance van, hidden amid the convoy of cars parked several yards away. Dozens of people gathered, huddled beneath a shield of black umbrellas, to pay their last respects.

McDaniel had been to a lot of funerals in his time—too many to count. And he'd always maintained that the best indicator of a life well lived was a death well mourned. So when he watched the presiding priest say a blessing and the casket lower as each of Julia's grief-stricken loved ones lined up to toss a single white lily into her grave, McDaniel knew, with utter certainly that Miles' mother had been a special woman.

"Looks like a nice party," Stokes said, as he adjusted the zoom on his Nikon and snapped a quick succession of action shots.

McDaniel shook his head. "Have a little respect for the dead, Brian."

"You wanna send some flowers?" Stokes asked with a sneer.

"I just don't see the point of keeping an eye on him while he's here."

"I don't buy his act," Stokes said. "Someone like Montego doesn't get to where he is, just to do an about-face. I'm telling you, this guy is smarter than the average crook." He peered through the binoculars dangling from his neck and surveyed the dispersing crowd. "If you ask me, I think it's a smoke screen."

McDaniel shrugged. "Maybe," he said, his heart heavy as he watched Miles' father—the last in a long line of the mourners—throw a handful of dirt into the hole where his wife's body lay. "Do you believe in God, Brian?"

Stokes rolled his eyes. "C'mon, Jason. Don't go and get all religified on me."

McDaniel chuckled. "I'm guessing you don't go to church, then."

"No, never," Stokes said, shaking his head. "You?"

"Yes, sir." McDaniel nodded. "Every week with my wife and kids—Bible study, prayer group, the whole nine yards."

"Really?" Stokes lowered his binoculars and looked at his partner, his expression one of surprise. "Why didn't I know that?"

Smiling, McDaniel's shrugged. "You never asked."

~

The repast, held at Miles' house, was peacefully uneventful. Friends and relatives gathered to enjoy some home-cooked food, give the Montego men their condolences, and remember Julia's life while celebrating her legacy.

All around him people sat in intimate cliques. Some laughed as they traded stories, others cried. In the dining room a small group of his aunts and cousins reminisced over old photos albums someone had brought. In the kitchen, the Leon women—who, without being asked, had taken on the role of unofficial hostesses—bustled about reheating a cache of potluck meals and washing a seemingly unending pile of dishes.

His house was full of people who knew his mother, who loved his mother, and who missed his mother. But in the coming days and months, their lives would return to the way they'd always been, while Miles would be forever trapped in this new normal—unsure of how to function, how to exist in a world where his mother didn't.

Eventually, the house began to empty. Ever the dutiful son, Miles smiled and expressed his gratitude to everyone who took the time to stop by. Martin and the rest of the crew were among the last to leave, followed shortly thereafter by Miguel Leon and his two youngest daughters. Vanessa, sensing Miles' exhaustion, volunteered to drive Caesar home so that Miles wouldn't have to make the trip across town.

Miles was eerily stoic as he helped his father to Vanessa's car and hugged them both goodbye. And he felt oddly numb as he headed back into the silence of his empty home and stared blankly at the wall, uncertain of what to do next.

"Miles?"

He looked up, startled to see Lydia Leon watching him with tears in her eyes. "Mrs. Leon. I didn't know anyone was still here."

"Miguel and the girls went ahead," Lydia explained. "I wanted to stay and make sure everything got cleaned up. You've got enough food in your fridge to last you 'til next Christmas," she joked weakly.

Miles' smile was perfunctory. "Thank you for everything."

Lydia started to leave, but turned back and sat down beside him. "Your mother was a beautiful woman," she said. "I saw the look in her eyes and felt the warmth in her heart when she saw you in church." Miles glanced at her and she smiled. "I haven't always been the easiest person when it comes to you. And I'm sorry for that. But I want you to know that I'm always praying for you." Lydia squeezed his arm. "Remember, you may not understand why God does certain things, but I promise you that it's all part of one big plan for your life. Just know that this family loves you."

"Thank you, Mrs. Leon." Standing, he gave her a hug. "That means a lot to me."

"You call if you need anything," she said.

Miles nodded. "I will."

Lydia let herself out and Miles found his way to the kitchen. Though he wasn't particularly hungry, he hadn't eaten all day and the lack of sustenance was starting to take its toll. Miles fixed himself a small plate and carried it to his office where he loosened his tie and sat down behind his desk. As he reached for his fork, his hand grazed the mouse resting beside his keyboard.

Instantly a slideshow of family photos he'd set for his screensaver began to play. Miles froze, caught off guard. Hot tears stung his eyes as he watched images of his mom, healthy and beautiful in years past, scroll across his computer monitor. Frantically, he pushed buttons and mashed keys, desperate to turn it off, but the images continued to scroll. They continued to taunt him, to remind him of what once was and what would never again be.

In one swift motion, Miles swept his arms across his desk and knocked everything to the floor with a loud crash. Angrily, he kicked his computer screen, stomping it until the stand was bent and the frame broken into pieces. Sweat beaded on his brow as his chest heaved beneath the unbearable weight of rage and sorrow.

With an agonized wail, he grabbed a nearby floor lamp and wielding the heavy base like a weapon, began to decimate everything in his path. He tore the artwork from the walls and threw the books from their shelves. He kicked over the furniture and smashed the potted plants. He beat the television and unhinged the cabinet doors.

Miles screamed and bashed and shattered and thrashed until there was nothing left to destroy. Until his voice gave in and his knees gave out. Until his mind went blank and his body went limp. Until all that remained was the inescapable pain of his immutable loss.

Part Three

Oh, Sweet Surrender

29

Vanessa stepped onto her front porch wearing a sultry smile and gave a flirtatious twirl so Miles could admire her from all angles. For her birthday celebration, she'd chosen an eye-catching red dress that hugged her curves in all the right places and a pair of black, strappy heels that accentuated her legs.

Miles' mesmerized gaze traveled the length of her body and back as she made her way toward him, "Uh oh! Okay," he said, nodding his approval. "Look at you. I'm loving it."

Vanessa giggled. "Thank you, baby."

"So, you ready for your birthday surprise?"

"Yes!" Vanessa had tried for the better part of a week to extract details of his mysterious plans, to no avail. The only thing he'd told her was where and when to be ready. But if the chauffeured Cadillac parked behind him was any indication, she knew this night was going to be one she would never forget.

"This is crazy, babe!" she said, her voice pitched high with excitement. She tilted her head. "But you know we could've just done something super simple like dinner."

"Well, it ain't too late to cancel," he shrugged. "Jimmy's is open 24 hours."

Vanessa laughed. "That's what we *won't* be doing," she said, grabbing hold of his hand. "Come on. Let's go!"

As if on cue, the driver got out and opened the door, greeting Vanessa with a smile and a tip of his hat as she climbed into the sedan's spacious backseat and waited for Miles to settle in beside her.

"*Now* will you tell me where we're going?" she asked.

"Nope." Miles shook his head. "Matter of fact," he said, pulling a silk mask from the inside pocket of his blazer. "Imma need you to put this on."

Vanessa laughed. "You can't be serious."

"No blindfold, no date," he warned, his grin mischievous.

"All right, fine," she relented as Miles positioned the soft fabric over her eyes. Gently, he fastened the elastic band around her head, careful not to tousle her coiffed hair.

Miles nodded at the driver. "Okay, we're ready."

Vanessa heard the engine purr and felt the smooth movement of the car when it eased away from the curb. She heard the click of the turn signal and felt the press of the brakes as the Cadillac reached the end of her street and their chauffeur navigated them out of her quiet neighborhood. She tried to envision their route in her mind, noting as they turned left, then right, then left again. But eventually she lost all sense of direction and had no choice but to sit back and enjoy the ride.

In time their speed slowed and the muffled swoosh of passing traffic was replaced by the sound of gravel crunching beneath their tires.

"We're here," Miles said as the car coasted to a stop.

"Where? Can I take this off now?"

"Not yet, not yet! Just hang on a sec." She heard Miles' door open and felt the leather seat beneath her shift as he exited. Seconds later, he was at her side. "Here, give me your hand," he said, guiding her out of the car.

"You know this is crazy, right?"

He chuckled. "Okay, walk this way some. Just follow the sound of my voice."

"It's windy," she noted, taking a few tentative steps forward. "Are there any steps?"

"No, baby. Don't worry. I got you."

She laughed, hardly able to stand the anticipation. "This is insane!"

"Okay, stand right there. You ready?"

"Are you kidding? Of course!"

Laughing, he removed the blindfold. "Happy birthday, baby."

Vanessa squealed with delight at the sight of a private jet parked just a few yards away. "Oh my gosh!" she gasped, clapping her hands elatedly as she took in the long red carpet leading from her feet to the stairs of the plane's open hatch. "Is this for real?" Before Miles could answer, she threw herself into his arms. "Thank you! Thank you! Thank you! Thank you!" she said, giving him a kiss, before turning on her heels and running toward the waiting aircraft.

Miles chuckled and followed her inside where they popped open a bottle of chilled champagne—awaiting them at Miles' request—and made a toast as the plane took off.

"I still can't believe I'm flying in a private jet," she said, shaking her head with disbelief. "Me! Vanessa Leon."

"Well, Ms. Leon. Would you like to know where I'm taking you for the weekend?"

"The weekend?" Her eyes grew wide with concern. "But what about my clothes? I didn't bring anything with me."

Miles' grin was devilish. "Don't worry," he said. "Everything's been taken care of."

Vanessa studied him, smirking suspiciously as she sat back against her seat and took a sip of her bubbly. "You were saying?"

"Tonight, I thought we'd keep it simple. Enjoy a romantic dinner at this great little spot I know. Have a few cocktails, look at the city lights, watch the sun set. And, if you're up for it, maybe hit up a lounge or two and get our dance on."

She smiled. "So far, I'm loving it."

"Then, tomorrow, we'll do some shopping and take in a few of the sites."

She nodded approvingly. "Okay..."

"And on Sunday, we'll head to Citi Field and watch the Yankees spank the Mets."

"Citi Field?" Vanessa's forehead wrinkled. "But that's in..." Her eyes grew wide with excitement as she slowly connected the dots. "New York! You're taking me to New York?"

Miles smiled. "I promised you I would."

"Oh, baby, thank you," she said, leaning across the narrow aisle to give him a kiss. Vanessa motioned around the luxurious cabin and then outside at their spectacular view of the world 40,000 feet below. "You couldn't have planned a more perfect evening."

"You know what I see?" Miles asked, motioning toward the window.

"What?" Following his gaze, Vanessa took a moment to admire the downy clouds and brilliantly orange hue of the open sky.

"I see God, baby."

"You do?"

"Only He could have created all this—a world full of hope and promise. A universe with no limits." Turning to look at her, Miles sighed. "I need to thank you. These past few months have been tough—really tough," he said. "And I'm not sure I would have made it through them without you."

It was true. The weeks following his mother's funeral had dragged by excruciatingly slow. Except for daily trips to check on his father, Miles had all but stopped living. As the days passed, his devastation turned into overwhelming sadness that, in time, morphed into a debilitating depression that eventually festered into a boiling anger that finally simmered into a deep-seated resentment toward the Lord.

People kept talking to him about God's grace and mercy, about His perfect sovereignty and divine will. They kept telling him to trust God's plan and to take comfort in the knowledge that his mom was now at peace. But the more they preached, the angrier Miles became.

Were it not for Vanessa's gentle prayers and sweet counsel he might've stayed lost in his own dark emotions. He might've given up and gone back to the man he used to be. But she continued to support him, without conditions or judgments. And on the days when he hated everything and everyone, including himself, she loved him enough for the both of them.

He smiled. "I've learned a lot."

"Yeah, like what?"

"Well, I've learned that I'm not as invincible as I thought I was. I learned life can be taken away from you just like that," he said with a snap. "I learned that God really and truly is in control of all of this." Miles studied her face intently. "But you know the most important thing I learned?"

Vanessa shook her head. "What?"

"I learned I never want to be alone," he said, bending down on one knee before her. "I never want to go back to life without you."

She gasped, covering her mouth as Miles pulled a black velvet box from his pocket. He opened it to reveal a stunning diamond engagement ring.

"Vanessa Leon, will you marry me?"

Tears filled her eyes. "Miles, ain't no question," she said, smiling as he slipped the promise of forever on her finger and sealed it with a kiss.

30

Miles was jarred awake by the shrill ring of his phone. He looked at the clock on his nightstand and then at the unfamiliar number that flashed across his caller ID. It was well past one o'clock on a Monday afternoon, yet he was still in bed, exhausted from his whirlwind weekend in New York with his new fiancée.

Sitting up, Miles shielded his eyes from the bright midday sun peeking through the slits in the drapes. "Hello?" he croaked, his voice hoarse with sleep.

"Yo, Miles. man, we got a situation."

"Marty?" Miles at up, suddenly alert. "What's going on?"

"Look, don't talk, just listen," Martin said, his tone matter-of-fact. "We got hemmed up, dogg. Me, Percy, Chris, Wikki—all of us, man. We locked up right now."

Sighing, Miles shook his head. "You gotta be kidding me."

"And to top it off, it was the Feds that got us," Martin said.

"The Feds?" Miles threw back the blankets and slung his legs over the side of the mattress.

"Yeah, they got our bail set at a half a million."

"What you want me to do?" Miles asked, already heading for his closet.

"I need you to get us outta here right now."

"All right, man. Hang tight. I'm on my way."

After posting their bond, Miles and the rest of the crew had convened to debrief. He glanced around the table and waited for someone to start talking. "So what happened?"

Martin spoke first. "Man, they came at us hard. I mean real hard, Miles. DEA vans all over the place, SWAT cars, guns. It was not good."

"What are the charges?" Miles asked.

Martin shook his head. "I don't even know. The indictment had all kinds of stuff in it, man. My lawyer's still working on sorting it all out."

"Okay, well, what about the spots? Was anyone dirty? Did they find anything?"

"Nah, man, but I'll tell you this, they tore up my place real good," Martin said, sitting back. "Thank God the only thing they found was a gun."

"Mine too," Wikki said. "They left my joint a mess."

"Those dudes bust my door down, Dogg." Percy folded his hands on top of the table. "They acted like they was looking for Bin Laden or something."

Martin nodded. "They was pressing us really hard, Miles."

"Pressing you?" he asked. "About what?"

"About you."

"Me?" Miles sat up. "What about me?"

Martin shrugged. "Man, they told me that I could get up and leave right then and there if I told them something juicy about you."

"Yup." Chris nodded. "They told me the same thing."

"This Agent McDaniel dude," Martin warned. "He got it real bad for you, Miles."

"Real talk," Percy said. "That dude offered to take me right back to my house and forget like any of this ever happened."

Miles nodded. "So, what'd you say?"

"I asked them if I could get ESPN in my cell," he said, smirking as the rest of the guys chuckled.

Miles turned to Martin. "What about you?"

"You really gotta ask me that?" Martin's forehead wrinkled with indignation. "After everything we've been through?"

Miles shook his head. "My bad, man. I'm sorry. I'm just trippin'."

"It's cool." Martin's nod was understanding. "Look, if you ask me, they were just fishing for something on you and using all of us as bait."

"Exactly," Chris said.

Wikki agreed. "You really need to watch your back, Dogg."

Miles took in all of their information with a shake of his head and a sigh. "All right, look, I want everyone to keep a low profile and stay out of their way until I figure this out. Got it?"

"Yeah, man, we got it," Martin said as the rest of the crew echoed the same.

Miles nodded. "Good."

31

Miles's office was a veritable sea of scattered receipts, old tax returns, contracts, bank records, brokerage statements, and every other important document he'd copied and filed away for the past ten years.

After his meeting with the fellas, he'd made an appointment with his lawyer, Clint Brown—a pit bull defense attorney who'd instructed him to bring in a host of paperwork so that they could get their ducks in a row in the event that Miles would have to prove his innocence in a court of law.

In the meantime, Clint had done a little digging and discovered that the DEA had been building a case against Miles and his crew for more than a year. In fact, they'd put together a special task force headed by none other than Jason McDaniel—a veteran agent who'd been credited for a number of high-profile drug busts over the course of his illustrious career. Working in tandem with San Jose's IRS Criminal Investigation unit, his team had gathered a mountain of incriminating evidence through wire taps and round-the-clock surveillance, though neither Miles nor his attorney would know exactly how serious the charges were until the indictment was handed down.

Miles checked his watch and grunted with frustration. He was supposed to be on the other side of town in less than twenty minutes, but he couldn't find the folder containing all of last year's financial filings. Ordinarily, he was extremely organized. As a business owner, he had to be. But his office had never quite returned to the same state of order it had been in prior to his emotional meltdown.

Though he'd spent the week afterward cleaning up the mess he'd made and replacing everything he'd smashed to bits, he'd never gotten around to fixing his files, and now nothing was where it was supposed to be.

Miles checked his watch again. Seventeen minutes and counting. He raked everything into a messy pile and scooping up as much of it as he could carry, headed for the door.

Miles was running so late that he was tempted not to answer his phone when it rang. But then he wondered if it was Clint with a few last minute instructions before their meeting or Martin with the latest developments in the case.

Using his free hand, he dug his cellphone out of his pocket and answered it just before the call went to voicemail. On the other end he heard what he thought was static and heavy panting.

"Who is this?" He sounded impatient, even to his own ears.

"Miles, it's Alyssa."

"Oh! Hey, Alyssa," he said, his tone decidedly friendlier. "What's up?"

Miles could only make out bits and pieces of the story relayed by Vanessa's youngest sister as she wept into the phone, but what little he did understand caused him to drop the pile of papers cradled in his arms and rush, as fast as he could, to San Jose's Regional Medical Center.

32

Miles felt an eerie sense of déjà vu as he stepped into RMC's lobby and made a beeline for the guest services kiosk.

Seated behind the desk was the same woman who'd given him directions when his mother had been admitted months earlier, though she didn't seem to recognize him as she looked up and smiled. "How can I help you, Sir?"

"My fiancée was in a car accident. They told me she was here."

"Her name?"

"Vanessa," Miles said. "Vanessa Leon."

She typed the information into her keyboard. "Well, I see she's been admitted," the woman said, reading the computer screen in front of her. "But it doesn't look like she's been assigned a bed yet." She handed Miles a visitor's badge. "There's a waiting room on the second floor. Just head to your left and—"

"It's okay," he said, cutting her short. "I already know the way."

Miles tried not to think the worst as he trotted around the corner and boarded an elevator with several others. But the second floor was the Intensive Care Unit, which meant if that's where Vanessa was going, her injuries were bad—life-threateningly bad.

The doors opened and his stomach churned with dread. Stepping off, Miles took the familiar walk down the wide, brightly lit corridor—passing the very room in which his mother had taken her last breath—and found the Leons seated together in a row of chairs along the wall.

Lydia looked wracked with worry as she hugged herself and stared at the scuffed linoleum floor. Julissa, nose red from crying, nervously twirled and untwirled a tattered tissue around her finger, while her father tried his best to comfort Alyssa who was sobbing quietly beside him.

"Miles." Miguel was the first to look up.

Miles met them as they stood. "What happened?"

"We don't know a lot of details at this point. Just that her car was struck by a truck. The driver ran a red light."

"Well, how is she?" he asked.

"She's still in surgery, but..." Lydia's eyes filled with tears as Miguel shook his head. "It's not good, Miles."

He sat down, suddenly nauseated.

"Let's not think the worst," Miguel counseled. "We just have wait. And pray."

"Mr. and Mrs. Leon?"

They all turned to see an older white gentleman dressed in blue surgical scrubs standing behind them. "I'm Dr. Mazza. I'm one of the trauma surgeons here at Regional Medical." He met Miguel and Lydia's pleading gazes with a heavy sigh. "Your daughter's in a coma."

Miguel wrapped an arm around his wife, who looked like she might collapse.

"Her injuries are significant," Dr. Mazza continued. "She suffered major internal bleeding as well as a collapsed lung and several broken ribs. However, what concerns us most is the severe head trauma she sustained. We've done all we can to stabilize her, but we won't know the extent of the damage or if additional surgeries will be required until the swelling in her brain goes down."

"What does that mean?" Miles asked. "Is she okay? Is she gonna wake up?"

"It's too soon to say." Dr. Mazza's tone was apologetic. "She'll be closely monitored in the ICU, but all we can do beyond this point is hope for the best."

"Hope?" Miles furled his lip with disgust. "You say hope and they say pray." He pointed at Vanessa's parents. "So, which one is it? Huh? Which one, cuz I need to know!"

"Come on. Take it easy." Miguel squeezed his shoulder, but Miles jerked away.

"I'm not gonna take it easy!" He turned his glare on Dr. Mazza. "What kind of surgeon are you? Coming out here, talkin' 'bout hope. I don't want hope I want answers!"

"We all do," Miguel said. "But it's in the Lord's hands now."

"The Lord's hands." Miles's scoff was indignant. "I'm sick and tired of hearing it's in the Lord's hands!" he shouted.

"Miles, stop!" Lydia pleaded as his outburst caught the attention of several people working at the nurse's station nearby.

"That's all I heard when my mother died—it's in the Lord's hands. But did that change anything? No!" His chest heaved with anger. "Tell me this, what good is it for everything to be in the Lord's hands if He's always out to lunch?"

Miles glanced around the circle at Vanessa's family and then back at Dr. Mazza, but no one offered any answers.

"Listen." Dr. Mazza's voice was calm, insistent. "We're going to do absolutely everything in our power to save her life. You have my word."

Miles shook his head. "I'm sorry, Doc, but that's not enough," he said, backing away. "That's just not enough."

"Where are you going?" Lydia asked.

"There's somebody I gotta talk to."

"Hang on a second, Son," Miguel pleaded. "Don't leave."

"I can't," he said stumbling out of the waiting room. "I just...I can't. I gotta go."

"Miles, wait!" Lydia called, chasing him around the corner and to the bank of elevators just in time to see the door close between them.

33

The swinging double doors leading into Evergreen Valley Church's sanctuary burst open with a loud bang as Miles stormed in and marched straight to the stained glass window at the end of the center aisle.

"Good! I'm glad You're here," he said, looking up at the floor-to-ceiling likeness of Christ praying in the Garden of Gethsemane. Miles had admired the window during each and every Sunday service he'd attended. It wasn't so much the artfully arranged bits of brightly colored glass that captivated him, as much as it was the power behind the story they depicted.

Faced with the prospect of unimaginable suffering, Jesus—Son of man—knelt before God Almighty to ask for a pardon—to plead for a divine reversal of fate. And Miles had come to do the same.

"We got some serious issues to talk about, You and me," he said, scowling as he pointed an accusatory finger at the image before him. "First of all, You took my mother from me and that just about killed me. But now You wanna take Vanessa too?" Miles shook his head. "Nah, Big Guy, that ain't gonna happen."

Sighing, he clasped his hands behind his neck. "Everywhere I turn people say You're the Way, You're the Truth, You're the Light. Just keep following You, keep trusting in You and everything will be all right. So, I do. I go to church, I read your precious little Book. I even drop stacks of hundreds every Sunday in that little velvet bag they pass around. I've changed!" Miles shouted, his voice echoing off the walls. "I'm a changed man! Can't You see that?"

Miles was met by nothing more than the sound of his own breathing. "Oh, my bad. Of course You can. You see everything, right?" He sneered. "So then what's the problem? What do You want from me?"

Tears pooled at the base of his eyes and trickled down his cheeks. "Look," he said, his voice cracking with emotion. "I know I haven't made You proud. How could I with everything I've done? But what happened to all these things I've been reading about? Grace, forgiveness, mercy."

Swiping at his tears, Miles hung his head. "Look, I'm a standup guy. If somebody has to pay for their sins, let it be me. I'm ready to take what I got coming," he said slapping his hands against his chest. "You wanna send me to hell? Book the flight! Just please, please—I'm begging You. Don't take Vanessa. Tell me what I gotta do to spare her life, and I'll do it. I'm done running. I'm done fighting."

Dropping to his knees, Miles lifted his tear-streaked face to the heavens and let out a tired sigh. "I surrender, Lord," he said, opening his arms wide, as peace, instant and certain, washed over him. "I surrender."

34

Snatching his toothbrush from its holder, Miles took a sharp turn out of his bathroom and into his closet where he ripped a couple of shirts from their hangers and stuffed them, along with a spare pair of jeans into an overnight bag.

He'd just received word from Miguel that Vanessa had been placed on a ventilator after her oxygen levels had dropped dangerously low overnight. Beyond that, she remained unresponsive as she lay alone in her hospital bed, quiescent and clinging to life.

As with his mother, there was nothing Miles could do. If he could turn back the hands of time and take Vanessa's place, he would. If he could fix her broken body with the wave of a magic wand or a wiggle of his nose, she would be safe with him right now—the picture of a vibrantly vigorous woman, very much alive and very much in love.

But in the end, all he could do was plead his case to God and, as a matter of course, lay aside his own will in a posture of reverence and obedience. He'd come to accept the fact that God might choose to save Vanessa or He might not. But either way Miles would be there by her side.

Cramming in enough clothes to last him a couple of days, he zipped up his bag and started for the door, when something caught his eyes. It was a photo of him and Vanessa taped to the corner of his closet mirror. One of the many self-portraits she'd snapped of them on the Golden Gate Bridge, the picture was, by far, one of his favorites of them. Her windswept hair and flushed face, his toothy grin and bright eyes. They were more than smitten, more than carefree. They were happy.

Miles peeled the photo off of the glass and stuck it in his pocket before heading downstairs and to his car. He debated whether he should go straight to the hospital or pay a quick visit to his father as he fastened his seatbelt and put his Bentley in reverse. But before he'd even backed out of the driveway, the street was suddenly flooded by police cruisers and SWAT vans, light flashing and sirens blaring. Dozens of officers, jumped out, guns drawn.

Through his rearview mirror, Miles watched as a man donning a blue DEA jacket and aviator sunglasses, stepped out of his car and, shielding himself behind his door, raised a bullhorn to his mouth. "Get outta the car!" His gruff command reverberated through the quiet streets of Miles' upscale neighborhood. "Get out of the car," he ordered again.

Unfastening his seatbelt, Miles slowly exited his car.

"Put your hands where I can see them and turn around!" the man shouted.

"Officer, what is all this—"

"Turn around!" he barked. "And walk backward."

Miles complied. Once he was several yards away from his car, the man ordered him to put his hands on his head and get down on his knees. Seconds later, three officers descended upon him and placed him under arrest. "You guys are making a big mistake," Miles said as one of them slapped a pair of cuffs on his wrists and roughly jerked him to his feet.

But they weren't interested in anything he had to say. Instead, they put him in the back of an unmarked squad car and hauled him to an interrogation room at the downtown precinct. Bare, but for a shabby table and two metal chairs, the room was stark white with harsh fluorescent lighting and surveillance cameras mounted in every corner.

Directly across from where Miles had been seated with one arm handcuffed to the leg of his chair, a large mirror took up most of the wall. On the other side, Agents Edgemond and McDaniel watched and waited.

Miles looked up at the sound of two detectives entering the room. One wore a black suit, the other a dress shirt and a tie. They were young—maybe mid-thirties, and clean cut. Both men sported badges on their waistbands and glasses. The solws of their dress shoes clicked in tandem against the tile floor as they approached.

The shorter one, whose curly hair fell in tight ringlets against his ears, dropped a box of files onto the table. "Mr. Montego. My name is Agent Carey and this is Agent Stokes," he said pointing at his partner. We're with the IRS." Pausing, he met Miles with a challenging stare. "Criminal Investigation Division."

Miles shrugged. "Yeah. So?"

"So we have a series of questions for you," Agent Carey said, pulling a folder from the box. "And we expect your full cooperation."

Smirking, Miles leaned back in his chair. "You could've just mailed me my tax refund."

Ignoring his quip, Carey tossed a stack of photos on the table and spread them out for Miles to see. "Do you know these guys?"

Miles glanced down at the surveillance images of Martin, Chris, Wikki, and Percy. "Yeah, they're friends of mine."

"How good of friends?" Stokes asked.

"Old friends," Miles said. "We went to school and grew up together."

Stokes narrowed his eyes. "Is that all you did together?"

"What's that supposed to mean?"

"It means that they've been indicted on drug charges," Agent Carey said. He shoved several documents at Miles. "It means that we've found these check stubs showing large payments from your company to each one of your buddies, here."

Stokes folded his arms across his chest. "It means that you look like you're in business with these guys, Miles. And if that's indeed the case, you're in a deep mess."

"I am a legitimate businessman," Miles said, his tone defiant. "And I don't do any illegal dealings of any kind." He pushed away the copies of the stubs and sat back. "So I wrote them some checks—big deal. Last I heard, that wasn't a crime."

"Well see now, you're wrong on that," Stokes said, perching on the edge of the table. "Writing checks can be a crime, especially depending on why they were issued."

"I'm a concert promoter. They invested in a few of my shows."

Agent Carey nodded. "Tell me, Miles. Do you know your friends' source of income?"

"No. And I don't care."

"Well, you should care," Stokes said. "Because their problems are quickly becoming your problems."

Miles smirked. "Oh yeah? And what kind of problems are those?"

"It's a problem when you use illegally gotten funds to finance even a legit business." Carey drew closer. "That makes all its gains and assets eligible for seizure by the IRS."

"I got nothing to hide." Miles looked from Carey to Stokes and back to Carey. "From you or anybody else."

"Miles, we're trying to give you a shot here," Stokes said. "A chance to save yourself a long and dirty investigation."

"Whatever man." Miles dismissed them with a wave of his hand. "Look, are we done here? Cuz I ain't got nothing else to say."

Sighing, Agent Carey closed the folder in his hands. "Hang tight. We'll be back." He and Agent Stokes gathered up their files and headed to an adjacent room where Edgemond and McDaniel had been observing their interrogation through the one-way mirror.

"What do you think?" Stokes asked.

McDaniel shook his head. "I think it's bad guy, one; good guys, zero."

"Yeah, well, not for long." Edgemond smirked. "I've been cracking punks like Montego for 30 years. If there's anything to tell, I'll get it out of him."

Carey handed him the file. "Be my guest."

"No, thanks," Edgemond said, reaching for the door knob. "I won't need it."

Miles threw his head back when Edgemond entered the room. "Look, man. I already told your partners that I'm not interested in answering no more of your questions. So ain't no point in y'all trying to pull that good cop, bad cop routine."

"First of all, I'm not a cop," Edgemond said, walking over to him and uncuffing his arm from the table.

Miles rolled his sore wrist back and forth. "Thanks."

"My name is Terry Edgemond. I'm an agent with the Drug Enforcement Administration," he said, straddling the chair across from Miles. "And I just want to talk."

"For what? You guys had your minds made up about me before you ever dragged me down here."

"I'll level with you," Edgemond said. "The evidence looks bad. We've got you associating with known traffickers, dealing in large amounts of cash, we even got you holding up two drug dealers at gunpoint in a San Francisco parking lot."

Miles thought back to the heated altercation between Martin, Chris, and Jesse. He dropped his head and sighed. "Man, that ain't even how it went down."

"Alright," Edgemond conceded with a shrug. "Then, how did it go down? I mean, that's why we're here, Miles. We want to get your side of the story." He reached for Agent Stokes' legal pad and pen, still resting on the table. "Let's take it from the beginning."

Miles sat for what felt like hours answering questions, explaining documents, filling in holes, and accounting for his whereabouts. Agent Edgemond grilled him mercilessly, oscillating between measured chumminess and crass petulance, in a determined effort to trip him up or catch him in a lie or coax him to confess to some level of wrongdoing.

"I don't know what else you want me to say." He threw his hands up, at a loss.

"Come on, kid. Give it a rest. Nobody's impressed by this song and dance of yours," Edgemond said, shaking his head. "You may have that pretty little girlfriend of yours snowed, but not me."

Miles glared. "Leave her out of this."

"Every Sunday like clockwork, you're in church—praying the prayers, singing the songs—but we both know you're no choir boy."

"What do you want from me, man?"

"I want specifics, Miles—names of your suppliers, drop-off points, warehouse locations, offshore accounts, everything."

"Like I told your boys, I'm a legitimate business—"

"I'm done playing games with you, son!" Edgemond shouted, banging his fist against the table. "You're gonna tell me what I want to know, or I'm gonna toss you in jail and throw away the key."

"Then, do it!" Miles' loud voice echoed off the bare walls as he met Edgemond's challenging stare with an unflinching gaze of his own. "I have a CPA who handles all my financial affairs and a lawyer who I'm sure will be more than happy to answer any more questions y'all may have. As for me, I'm done talking," he said with a stubborn tilt of his chin. "If you're gonna charge and arrest me, hurry up and do it so I can bail out and go on with my day. But if not." Miles shrugged. "Then, show me the door."

Stokes shoved his hands in his pockets as Edgemond rejoined him, Carey and McDaniel in the next room. "So what do you wanna do?"

"He lawyered up" McDaniel said. "There's not much we *can* do."

Carey scoffed. "I think we should throw him in a holding cell for 72 hours. Maybe a few nights in jail will incentivize him."

"That could work." Stokes nodded.

"I don't know." McDaniel looked at Agent Edgemond and shrugged. "Maybe he's that squeaky clean choir boy after all."

Edgemond studied Miles intently for a few moments. "I think you're right," he said, turning to the others with a sigh. "Cut him loose. He's free to go."

35

Vanessa looked peaceful as she lay alone in her hospital room. Were it not for the rhythmic beep of her heart monitor and the loud hum of her ventilator, she would have looked as though she was napping—dreaming of sunshine and rainbows and happily ever after.

"I'm sorry I'm so late, baby," Miles said. Crossing the room, gave her a soft kiss on the forehead before kneeling beside her, taking her hand in his. "Listen, I'm gonna try a prayer. So don't laugh at me, okay? You know I'm new to this."

Vanessa continued to lay, motionless.

"Dear God, what can I say?" Miles began. "I give up. I finally figured out that You are who You say You are and that I can't do nothing without You." Eyes closed, he grinned. "I know now that You run this whole thing. And that everything I have belongs to You—including Vanessa. I come before You today, humbling asking—no begging You, God. Please, please spare her life. Please allow her to come out of this coma and restore her health. I'm here to do or say, Lord, whatever You ask of me."

Miles sighed. "I know I don't have much to offer You, but what I have and all that I am is Yours. I want You in my life. I want You in my heart. And I promise to be as faithful to You as I possibly can. I love You, and I pray all these things in Your name, Christ Jesus. Amen."

36

"Good morning, Church!" Pastor Tim said, greeting his congregation with a jubilant smile from behind his pulpit. "If you've got your Bibles, say, 'Got it!'"

"Got it!" They all replied in unison.

"Good. Turn with me to James, chapter one. And this is the Word of the Lord: 'Consider it pure joy, my brothers and sisters, whenever you face trials of many kinds, knowing that the testing of your faith develops perseverance.' How many of you know that we must allow perseverance to have its work in our lives, because God uses that to complete us and mature us?"

Pastor Tim nodded as most of those in attendance raised their hands. "Well, this morning, I'm looking at a family who went through a beast of a trial." He pointed to the front row. "Leon Family, would you please stand up?" Miguel, Lydia, Julissa, Alyssa, and Miles obliged, smiling at Vanessa as she rose from her seat.

"Church, we prayed faithfully for God to do a miracle, and He did just that. Vanessa is here and she's healthy, and I just want to give God some glory!"

The sanctuary automatically filled with shouts of rejoicing and praise as the members of Evergreen Valley Church celebrated Vanessa's miraculous recovery.

She lay in a coma for more than two weeks with little sign of improvement. And Miles remained by her side the entire time. Though he didn't know until the moment she finally stirred and opened her eyes that she would be okay, he had found peace in the understanding that God was faithful, His way perfect, and His grace sufficient.

"Hallelujah!" Pastor Tim said, as their cheers died down and everyone took their seats. "Now the Bible also says, 'Today is the day of my salvation that now is the acceptable time to receive the Lord Jesus Christ as your Savior." His eyes swept over the congregation. "I sense that there may be someone here today who would like to confess Jesus Christ as their Lord and Savior. If that's you and you want to say, 'Yes! I'm ready to open my life to You today, Lord,' would you make your way to the altar?"

"Excuse me, Pop," Miles said, moving down the row.

Vanessa reached for his arm. "Baby, where are you going?"

"I'll be right back," he said. "I made a promise to Someone that I gotta keep."

She let him go and watched him shuffle sideways past her family and into the aisle. Lydia grabbed Vanessa's hand, tears springing to both their eyes, as he made his way up the stage steps and into Pastor Tim's open arms as the church erupted into thunderous applause.

EPILOGUE

THREE YEARS LATER ...

Yo, Fellaz!

I hope all of you are in the best of health and spirits. I hope you're staying outta trouble, too. Cuz, I know how y'all like to wild out. I can't tell you how much I miss you all. I can't imagine how hard it is in there.

As for me, what can I say? I guess God has a sense of humor! So much has happened over these past few years. It's been crazy, but all to the good, you know?

It's truly a new season. Some days I still can't believe I turned in my playa card and finally wifed Vanessa. But, man, I wouldn't go back for anything in the world. I was born to love her.

She's doing great, by the way. She got a new job teaching at a small Christian academy in Palo Alto and is enjoying every minute of it. Meanwhile, I graduate in a couple of weeks. Who'd have ever thought ya boy would be a college grad!

Anyway, we both can't wait for you to get home. Good news is, you're short timers, now. Just a little ways to go and it's all over, yo!

Remember everything we talked about at our visits. God is good and He is faithful and I promise that He's inside those walls just as much as He is out here.

> I sent some money to your books already. It should be enough to last you until you get out. I love y'all and I can't wait to see you guys on the outside, in real clothes.
>
> Steaks are on me!
>
> Love, Respect & Blessings,
>
> Miles
>
> P.S. You guys are gonna be uncles soon, so straighten up! I don't want my kid around no knuckleheads, ya dig?

Miles smiled as he stuffed his letter to Martin into an envelope and quickly addressed it. Tossing it atop a pile of mail on his desk ready to be sent out, he checked his watch, and noting the time, grabbed his Bible and notebook and rushed out of his office.

"Hey, how are you," he said, greeting Melinda, one of the church secretaries, heading in the opposite direction down the corridor.

"I'm great! Did Vanessa get my message about rescheduling the monthly Women's Bible Study?"

"I'm not sure. But you know what? I'll have her call you a little later this afternoon."

She smiled. "Perfect, thanks."

"Sure thing," he said, turning around just as he bumped into one of the members of the Men's Ministry. "Rey! What's good, man? Imma see you here Thursday night, right?"

Shaking his hand, Rey nodded. "Most definitely."

"That's what I'm talking about," Miles said, continuing down the hallway. He followed it around a corner and up a flight of stairs to an interior door. Opening it, he walked across a carpeted platform and, placing his Bible on the podium, looked upon the waiting congregation.

Instantly, his eyes fell on Vanessa seated in the front row, her hands resting affectionately on her belly. "Good morning, Church! I'm Pastor Miles." He smiled. "And today, we're gonna talk about change..."